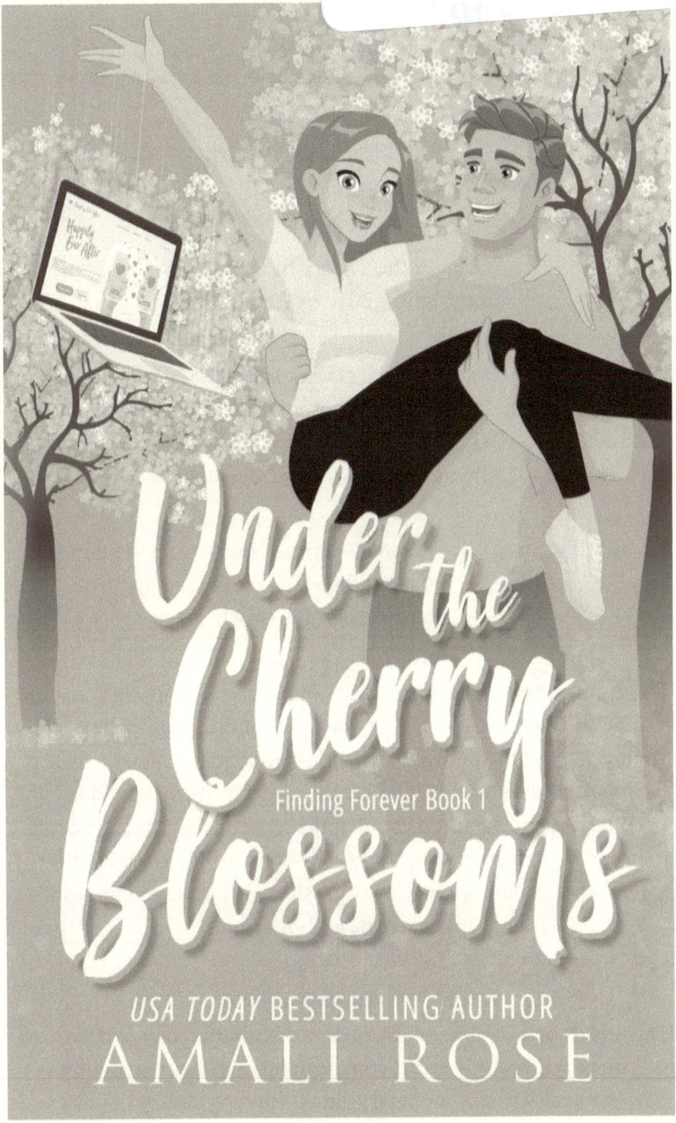
Happily Ever After
Under the Cherry Blossoms
Finding Forever Book 1
USA TODAY BESTSELLING AUTHOR
AMALI ROSE

Under the Cherry Blossoms

Finding Forever Book 1

USA TODAY BESTSELLING AUTHOR

AMALI ROSE

This book is for everyone who has ever let fear hold them back.
Be brave. Be strong. Be you.

"I learned that courage was not the absence of fear, but the triumph over it. The brave man is not he who does not feel afraid, but he who conquers that fear."

Nelson Mandela

Synopsis

She doesn't want a happily ever after. She just wants a happy ending. Cue the online dating app…

It may have begun as a drunken attempt at a virtual booty call, but when Ben Mackinnon sets his sights on the intentionally lovelorn Skye Emery, he pulls out all the stops in an attempt to convince her that romantic ideals like soulmates and forevers really do exist.

Skye doesn't want to believe a word. But try as she might, she can't help but catch feelings for the sexy, reformed ladies man. It's his corny sense of humour that does it—along with his self confidence, and of course, his _very_ dirty mouth.

Their relationship blossoms, and just as these two lovebirds start to believe they've beaten all the odds, Ben's unresolved past becomes a barrier that sends him reeling and Skye running for the door.

The aftermath leaves Skye with two—well, _three_— choices: fight for her happily ever after, accept that her relationship with Ben was just one booty call too many, or eat her weight in ice cream.

While the ice cream option seems enticing, Skye already knows what she needs to do…

2 *003*

My head feels foggy as I watch my father from my cross-legged position on the floor where I'm sitting, still trying to make sense of everything that has happened tonight.

"Skylah?"

I blink once. Twice.

"Skylah." My father's voice is louder, more insistent this time, and I see him crouched down in front of me. He's holding my hands in his, but I can't seem to feel them. The sense of security that normally follows his touch has vanished.

"Honey, this is for the best, you'll see. Your mom and I have been so unhappy. We need this."

As the words leave his mouth, I hear a glass smash on the tiled floor, just outside the bedroom door, and hear my mother's footsteps fade away as she rushes down the hall.

Sighing, my father stands up, his broad shoulders slightly hunched, and a look of frustration crosses his face. Closing his eyes, he takes a breath and seems to regroup as the sound of his phone buzzing with a text fills the air.

Looking down and pulling up the message, a slow smile lights his face, all sense of frustration gone.

It's her, I realize with horror and I feel a single tear escape. Brushing it away furiously before he can notice, I watch as he slides his phone in his back pocket and resumes packing with a renewed vigour.

Moments later, he zips his suitcase closed and approaches me.

"C'mon, honey, walk me out," Dad says, holding his hand out to me. I take it hesitantly. There's no way I can stop this so refusing seems petty, and I allow him to lead me to the front door.

"I'll call when I get home, okay?"

Home. This is your home, I want to scream. Here with me and Mom! But I don't. I nod mutely and let him draw me into a tight hug. All too soon, he pulls away and with a last brush of his hand across my cheek, he turns and walks out the door. I watch him make his way down the front path, hop into his car, gun the engine and drive off down the street. The hand I had raised to wave goodbye, drops quickly back down to my side. There's no point. He never looked back.

CHAPTER ONE

"Ugh, shit." The words fall from my lips as I trip over the cushion left on the floor with all the grace of a stumbling hippopotamus. Okay, maybe that last glass of wine wasn't the smartest idea I've ever had. As I pull myself up I search for my kindle and sigh in relief as I spot it safe on the couch. I reach down and pick it up as I make my way to my bedroom, ready to curl up and enjoy my latest book boyfriend and this wine buzz I have going on.

After getting ready for bed I am snug and settled, devouring the filthy words on the screen with the enthusiasm of someone who has clearly not enjoyed any sexy times in a ridiculously long while. As my eyes eat up the words, my hand unconsciously smooths its way down my body, seeking relief from the tension pulsing in my core. As my fingers slide through the wetness, I groan softly. Grazing my clit lightly, a shiver escapes me. I am so worked up it's only a matter of minutes before my teasing fingertips have worked their magic and I am moaning my release.

I sigh as I roll over thinking how too many of my nights are ending this way. I've almost forgotten what it feels like to have an actual guy touch me, and frankly, I'm ready to give myself the "it's not you, it's me speech". I think about the advice my best friend Cassidy gave me the other day; online dating. I mean there's no shame in it these days, right? We're all busy, it's a perfectly respectable way to meet people. And it works. I've seen the testimonials and surely, they wouldn't lie. Right?

While I still retain a bit of liquid courage, courtesy of all the wine I drank tonight, I grab my phone and google "most successful dating sites". It would seem Happily Ever After is the site of choice for all the despera... I mean, hopeful singles out there. I stifle a laugh at the name. I'm not looking for a happily ever after. Just a happily ever orgasm. So, before I lose my nerve, I pull up the website and click on the 'create an account' button. Ten minutes later, I have completed my profile and set it loose into the online dating world. My smiling face gazes out at me from the phone screen and I can't help looking at myself with pity. A sense of dread settles in my stomach as I send out a silent prayer to the dick-pic gods. Please no delfies. Or, you know, at least make them dicks worthy of my admiration. Oh god, what have I done?

BEEEEEP.

I sigh quietly as I reach to open the microwave and pull out the dinner for one as Cassidy continues her rant in my ear. "Seriously, Skye, I'm not sure how much longer I can stay there. The work is boring as fuck and the people are even worse! How can I be expected to work under those conditions? I'm not getting any sleep at night because I'm falling asleep out of boredom every day!"

I try to hold in a giggle as I listen to Cassidy complain about her job in office administration. Unfortunately, the result is an unattractive snort-giggle that alerts her to my mirth. "Well, I'm glad you find my pain so funny, loser!" she shrieks, and I can feel her glowering through the phone, which causes me to lose any pretence and I burst out laughing.

"It's work, Cass, it's not supposed to be fun. It's just the eight hours we have to get through every day to get to the fun stuff."

"Speaking of the fun stuff, you wanna go out tonight? Cocktails and tapas?" The change in Cassidy's voice is immediate and if I didn't know her so well, would be slightly disconcerting. But after ten years of friendship I am used to her swift mood changes and at times like this, I am grateful for them. Her work diatribes are becoming a daily occurrence.

"I would but I've got myself a hot date tonight. Ben and I agreed to chat at 8 o'clock." I listen as Cassidy whoops loudly on the other end of the phone, mumbles something about sexting and starts to sing "bow chika wow wow."

I roll my eyes at her outburst, but I can't help the smile that spreads across my face. Cass is my opposite in every way. The yin to my yang, the Scary Spice to my Baby Spice. She is the dark to my light and I couldn't imagine my life without her. She has also seen me despair over the long list of less than desirable men that have replied to my online profile and encouraged me to persevere. Cassidy claimed the answer to my sex drought was only a click away, and don't think she didn't proclaim her triumph loudly when Ben Mackinnon appeared in my Happily Ever After mailbox. Sexy as hell and, if his messages are anything to go by, sweet, smart and funny; he ticked all my boxes and then some. And I'm not going to lie; the fact that he didn't send me a dick pic within the first ten minutes had definitely worked in his favor.

"Okay, okay, okay, enough!" I laugh as I cut Cassidy off mid-chika. "I have fifteen minutes to scarf down this meal before it's B-time so I've got to go. I'll talk to you tomorrow, okay?"

"B-time? Really? I sincerely worry about your cool cred sometimes, you nerd. But that's a topic for another day. Later, Skyballs, and remember, two hands on your phone at all times, young lady!"

I groan as Cassidy hangs up on me and I place my phone on the kitchen counter. Tucking a strand of my long brown hair behind my ear, I pick up my fork and dig into my lean cuisine. After a quick glance at the clock I see it's ten minutes to eight, and feel the butterflies start. Truth be told, I'm completely out of practice with this whole dating thing. My list of exes did nothing to change my mind and convince me that a happily ever after was in my future, and I had forgotten about this complex mix of excitement and fear which left you unsure if you were giddy or nauseous!

Placing my dishes in the dishwasher, I move to the couch and settle in for what I hope will be a long chat. Because chatting to Ben has become the highlight of my day, and while I probably should, I feel absolutely no shame in admitting that. The last month talking to him has been fun and easy; I find myself almost craving the contact with him. He has tried to convince me to meet him in person a handful of times but I've resisted. There is safety in where we are now, in the protection that the phone screen affords me. I started this online thing to find someone to have fun with. Someone who can scratch my metaphorical itch anytime it tingles, but the longer I talk to Ben, the more I can see myself falling for him and I can't let that happen. My head understands this but as my phone dings and my heart begins to pound, it's clear that my heart might not be on the same page. Ugh, someone needs to give me a stern talking to. I am a twenty-eight-year-old grown woman, not a giddy, giggling preteen. Then again, I haven't gotten laid in a while, so I give myself a pass.

Ben: You there, beautiful?
Skye: Yep. How was your day?

Riveting, I know. Have I mentioned I'm out of practice?

. . .

Ben: Good, busy. One of the systems crashed so we spent the day trying to clean up that shit storm. I hope yours was better?

Skye: I'm not even going to pretend to understand the computer stuff lol but it sounds like a rough day, so I'm sorry. I almost feel bad telling you that I had a fantastic day, I got a promotion!

As happy as I was about the promotion, it was bittersweet. My boss, Juliet, had informed me that she wanted to take a step back from running Books & Beans, the bookstore slash coffee shop that she owned. So, she was promoting me to manager, and while I was incredibly excited about the chance to have more responsibility, and my mind was bursting with ideas, I was also slightly terrified at the prospect of failing.

Ben: That's incredible news! We have to celebrate. What about dinner on Friday night?

My hand freezes over the phone keyboard. I'm not ready for this, it's too soon. I mean, I know that realistically it stopped being too soon about two weeks ago (according to Cassidy "Bow Chika Wow Wow" Jensen, anyway) but I'm not sure I'm ready to take that next step yet. My phone vibrates in my hand, bringing my gaze back to the screen.

Ben: Baby, I'm sorry, I have to go, work just called and they need me back there. I'll make some reservations for Friday and get back to you, okay? I'm really happy for you.

Well shit. I guess I'm meeting Ben.

CHAPTER TWO

The week sped past in a blur of chaos. There was so much to do at B & B to ensure everything was ready for Juliet to leave, and I was still struggling with the idea of losing the safety net I had with her presence. While I adored her, and was so excited for this next stage of her life, I was terrified of letting her down and destroying all that she had built. Juliet, however, had no such qualms.

"My sweet Skylah, you will be fine. You need to stop worrying. You know everything there is to know," she huffed exasperatedly. It is Friday afternoon and it would seem that my third confirmation of the bakery delivery times has used up the last of Juliet's usually limitless patience. Considering I have met the delivery truck every morning for the last three years, I am prepared to admit she has a point.

"Don't you have a date tonight? Why don't you head home early, my love?" I glance over and take in Juliet's soft smile. This woman has been like a second mother to me and I don't know how I'm going to get along without seeing her every day. Straightening my back, I return her smile.

"Fine. I can take a hint, I'll get out of your hair and give you some peace." I listen as she chuckles softly and waves me out the door.

"Go! Call that crazy Cassidy. Maybe she can calm those nerves that I know you're trying to hide." I roll my eyes but I can't deny her claim and she knows it.

"CJ is at the spa with Mom today, it's her birthday," Layla, Cassidy's little sister who works part time at Books & Beans, informs me as she walks over to join us.

"Oh, that's right, I remember her mentioning it to me earlier this week. That's probably better anyway, I think she'd just wind me up more rather than calm me down." Layla giggles out an adorable snort of agreement as I give both her and Juliet a kiss on the cheek before grabbing my purse from under the counter and heading for the door.

"Have a great night, ladies. Wish me luck, and I'll let you know how it goes tomorrow, 'kay? Bye!"

As I stroll home the nerves hit me full force. As stressful as this week has been, it has also offered a good distraction. Ben has also been busy at work, the system crash on Monday had proved to be more serious than anyone had expected, so our messages had been brief and fewer than either of us would have liked. Now, however, I have nothing to divert my thoughts from my upcoming date with a guy who could quite possibly make my life very difficult. My chest tightens as I think about coming face to face with Ben. I really don't want to mess this up. Our online relationship has been uncomplicated so far, but in reality, I'm quite a shy person and I dread the idea that things could feel awkward and forced. I pick up the pace, eager to get home, sink into a hot bath and hopefully relax a bit. Tonight will be fine. No, better than fine, it's going to be amazing. I inhale and exhale that mantra all the way home.

❦

Three hours later, I step out of the Uber and try to calm my nerves. Looking up at the elegant sign above the door, I confirm that this is indeed Petite Assiette d'Amour. Taking a deep breath, I straighten my spine, stand tall and head into the little restaurant Ben has chosen for our date, trying to convey a confidence I don't particularly feel. Inside is cosy and immediately envelopes you in a warm atmosphere that invites comfort and intimacy. Another tick for Ben. As I walk up to the hostess station I'm greeted by a stunning blonde who throws me a welcoming smile.

"Good evening, what name was your reservation under?" she asks.

"Uh, it should be under Mackinnon, thank you," I reply as I smooth down the skirt of my red dress. It flares out and hits me mid-thigh, showing off a healthy amount of leg. Standing at 5'2" my legs may not be the longest, but years of walking around NYC has kept them slim and toned, and I can appreciate the stares they garner.

"Right this way, Mr. Mackinnon is already seated." I follow behind and as I glance ahead and spot Ben's chiselled profile, my anxiety peaks. I'm suddenly comparing myself to the hostess' made-up perfection. I rarely wear much makeup, just a dab of mascara and eyeliner to bring out the green of my eyes and a slick of gloss on my full lips. But suddenly, I feel lacking. You can do this, I tell myself firmly. You are going to have a great time tonight. He will have a great time tonight. And. You. Will. Not. Throw. Up. I almost snort out loud as this thought runs through my head, and I wonder if Ben is experiencing the same kind of nerves. Although, from where I'm standing, it doesn't look like it. Okay, a tick in the minus box for Ben.

As we approach, I practically drink Ben in from across the room. He has his phone out and is examining it with a serious expression on his face until his lips quirk with a small smirk that brings out a mischievous gleam in his dark brown eyes. It's noticeable even from this distance. His carelessly tousled brown hair, paired with the dark denim jeans and black dress shirt he's wearing is the perfect combination of casual and care. When we near the table, Ben notices us approach and unfolds his six-foot-plus frame out of his chair and with a grin spreading across his gorgeous face, he reaches out to greet me, seeming to not even notice the blonde beauty beside me, and pulls me into a warm hug.

"Finally."

I laugh lightly, acknowledging my reluctance to meet in person, while subtly breathing in the scent of his cologne which manages to be both spicy and sweet at the same time.

"It's great to finally meet you too. This place seems wonderful, you did good!"

"Thanks. I have to admit, my friend Mason recommended it, but it really is perfect, isn't it?" Ben smiles as though recollecting something. "He's a total workaholic, but it means he knows all the best restaurants from all his business meetings, so I keep him around."

A laugh escapes me as I settle back into my chair and we sit staring at each other. The air is suddenly tinged with self-consciousness and we both seem to be at a loss as to what to say, so the silence stretches. Dread settles in my stomach as all my fears seem to be coming to fruition.

We both speak simultaneously. "I hope you didn't have trouble finding the place."

"So, were you able to sort out the issues at work?"

And just like that, the tension dissipates as we both share a soft laugh over the absurdity of our nervousness.

This one moment seems to bring us to our senses and we launch into conversation, talking about everything from our favorite music and foods (him: The Rolling Stones/pizza, me: Taylor Swift/lasagna) to our political beliefs (both of us: they're all hopeless and we're screwed). The night flies by in a blur of laughter, good alcohol and even better conversation. My heart ratchets up every time Ben smirks at me and while our conversation has been fun and easy for the most part, he has thrown enough suggestive comments my way for me to know that that mouth of his is trouble. The kind of trouble that makes my thighs clench in anticipation.

The check is being brought over before I know it and I can't help wishing the night didn't have to be over.

"How about we share an Uber home?" Ben asks as he pulls out his phone and brings up the app.

"Perfect," I reply, thinking how well this night has turned out and how grateful I am that I took the chance and didn't chicken out.

By the time we have finished inside the restaurant, the Uber is outside waiting. Climbing in, we circle back to our heated discussion about the best movies of all time, both of us passionately defending our choices.

"Dirty Dancing is a classic. A true classic!" I exclaim. "There are millions, hell maybe even billions, of people who can quote it. Who can quote The Big Lebowski?"

"Fuck it, Dude. Let's go bowling," Ben throws back at me.

Wait, what? Is he asking me out again? My eyes widen and I'm not really sure how to respond. His brown eyes are warm and a smile is playing on his full lips as he watches me, and suddenly I forget all about my pro Dirty Dancing arguments. Right now, the only thing I want to debate is his place or mine.

"The Big Lebowski." This highly unromantic statement brings me back to earth with a crash, and I try to regain my wits and remember what he was saying.

"That's a quote from The Big Lebowski. So, you see, plenty of people can quote it." He looks at me with a cocky little smirk that makes me want to roll my eyes. Smartass.

I look out the window as the car comes to a stop and realize we've arrived.

"Consider yourself lucky we're here," I say as we climb out of the car. "I was just about to launch into a medley of all the hits from one of the most iconic soundtracks of all time. You know, from the best movie of all time." He clutches his chest and pulls a face of devastation.

"Oh. No. However will I survive?" he retorts in a monotone voice. "I'm sure the bleeding ears would have been so much fun." I laugh at his response, and am trying to come up with a smart comeback when he continues, "but we could always finish this next week? I've never had a girl serenade me before. I think you have to agree to see me again just so I can tick that off my bucket list."

I smile a huge, completely not-playing-it-cool smile.

"I'd like that, let's do it. Although, be prepared, because I am a truly horrible singer."

"I doubt anything your mouth does would be horrible," Ben replies as he leans down, slanting his mouth over mine. Reaching up, he slides his hand into my hair and tugs firmly, repositioning my head so he is able to deepen the kiss. I feel a rush of heat spread through my body as his tongue wrestles with mine, and I can't help but wonder if it will be as skilled when exploring other parts of my body. I feel myself get lost in Ben's touch, the pull on my hair, the way his tongue slides against mine. This kiss is unlike any I've experienced before but also so familiar, as if I've been kissing this man all my life. Then, as suddenly as it started, the kiss is over and Ben is walking back toward the car. As he bends down to get in, he looks back and says, "We'll talk tomorrow, okay? Now, head inside so I know you got in safely."

I smile and retort, "So bossy."

And as I turn to unlock the door, I hear him reply, "You'll get used to it."

I roll my eyes and head inside with a smile on my face.

CHAPTER THREE

"Skye fucking Emery! Wakey wakey!"

I'm dragged ruthlessly from my slumbering oblivion by the sound of kitchen cupboards slamming and a screeching voice intent on rousing me awake. Refusing to give in to these terrorist tactics, I roll over and stick my head under my pillow. Cassidy will not be thwarted however, and the next thing I know she is body slamming me into the mattress with a maniacal laugh.

"Skyballs! C'mon! I need all the details! Did he pound your pussy? Batter dip the corn dog? Did you do the boom boom? Tell me everything!"

I move the pillow away and throw a what-the-fuck look over my shoulder.

"Oh my god, Cass, what is wrong with you? Batter dip the corn dog? Seriously? And I want my key back, you jerk." Her only response is a loud laugh which stops as suddenly as it started while she throws me her infamous puppy-dog eyes.

"Skye. I don't mean to alarm you, but you have no food in the place. You need to take me out and feed me."

Groaning, I crane my neck to see the alarm clock and note that it's only 8:15 in the morning.

"Cassidy Jensen, I know for a fact that there is a kitchen full of food in there. And what the hell are you doing out of bed before 10am on a Saturday morning?"

"Nope, there's only healthy shit in there, I want pancakes. And I'm up because my pathetic excuse for a best friend never messaged me last night to tell me how her date with the man-meat went. Now get your ass up, you're taking me to Monroe's."

I stare at the ceiling, silently debating whether I want to humor her or kick her butt out when she makes the decision for me, lifting the mattress and watching as I tumble to the ground with a loud, "oomph."

"Now, Skyballs." And she walks out my bedroom door without a backward glance.

&

As we walk down the steps to the sidewalk, Cassidy links her arm in mine and we start the three-block walk toward Monroe's, our favorite diner.

"So, seriously babes, how did it go?" She squeezes my arm reassuringly and waits me out, knowing that I need a minute to verbalize my thoughts.

"It was good, Cass. Really good. I mean, a bit awkward to begin with, but once we had a laugh over how ridiculous it was to be so nervous, the ice was broken and it felt just like talking to him online."

"But…" Cassidy prods me.

I pause as I decide how to continue. When Ben drove away last night I was on a high. Almost drunk on the giddy feeling his kiss had left me with. It wasn't until later when I was lying in bed alone, that I realized the night had not ended the way I had planned. I wasn't sure what to make of that.

Monroe's appears up ahead and my stomach grumbles almost instinctively. "Let's eat and then talk, yeah? I may need to drown my sorrows in some maple syrup."

"Maple syrup? Fuck yeah!" Cassidy picks up speed, dragging me through the entrance.

I glance around the bustling diner looking for an empty seat when our friend Wyatt, who also happens to be our favorite waitress, rushes past and calls out over her shoulder, "Free booth down at the very back!" I throw her a grateful smile and we head in the direction she indicated.

Taking a seat, I watch as Cassidy throws herself into the booth like an excited toddler and snatches up the menu.

"Why do you even bother? We both know you're going to get pancakes with ice cream, maple syrup and a side of bacon. It's what you always get."

"Are you insinuating that I'm predictable, Emery?"

Even the idea of Cassidy being predictable is laughable and I dismiss the idea with a snort.

"I'm just saying let's save time and order what we

both already know we're going to get." With impeccable timing, Wyatt appears, pen poised ready to take our order.

"Hit me with it, cuties."

"Skye finally went out with McSausage last night," Cassidy replies.

"Oh my god, how did it go?!" Instead of taking our order, Wyatt is now sitting opposite me with an expectant look on her face. That is, until she gives Cassidy a side-eye look. "Wait, McSausage?"

"Oh please, we all know he's too hot not to be packing a huge pork sword." Turning to me she continues, "Confirm or deny please."

Ignoring her, I turn and give my attention to Wyatt. "I'd like French toast please, Wyatt, and the biggest chocolate milkshake you can possibly bring me."

Looking between the two of us she seems unsure how to proceed until Cass also gives her order. Wyatt sighs and gets up, ready to walk away. "You owe me details, Skylah!" Then she races off, hopefully to put in our orders.

"Okay, Balls, talk," Cassidy demands.

Cringing inwardly at the use of this particular nickname, I opt for the direct route and reply, "We didn't fuck."

"Right. Okay. Well that blows. I mean, not literally, obviously, but you know what I mean. You said it went well though, does it matter if you didn't belly bump?"

"But that was the whole point of this, right? To get intimate with something other than my own hand? I couldn't even seal the deal, I mean, he didn't even try!"

Cassidy sighs emphatically and I can feel every bit of her frustration in that deep exhalation.

"Talk me through this, Skye, because from what I'm understanding, you've met a nice, smart, hot guy who is actually into you. Who hasn't messed you around at all in the month that you've known him. A guy that had to chase you down before you would actually meet him. But he did. He did that for you, and I'm not even joking when I say there's a part of me that hates you right now. I think he's one of the good ones, and there's not many of them around, so I kind of want to tell you to get the fuck over yourself and just go with it." Running out of breath as she finishes her spiel, Cassidy slumps forward onto the table dramatically.

I try to quiet the noise in my head that her speech created and figure out how to put my thoughts into words. I know it doesn't make sense. I'm the girl who reads the romance novels. The one who tells my friends to never give up on love because their happy ending is out there and I absolutely, wholeheartedly believe that. For some reason though, I can't have that same faith in myself. I watched my father walk out when I was thirteen years old and I swear it almost broke me. The man that was supposed to love me more than anyone, walked out that door and he didn't look back, not even once. I'm not sure I could survive that again.

"I don't need him to be one of the good ones, Cass. I need him to bend me over a table and fuck me until I black out." And in a case of the worst possible timing, a guy in his early twenties walking past stops in his tracks and, as if in slow motion, turns to look at us. Leaning down, he offers me his hand and says, "Hi, I'm Michael, might I be of some assistance?"

"No, you might not be, Creepy McPervert! Move along," Cassidy spits out, as I feel my face turn a distinct shade of red. I'll just die now, shall I? "Well, Emery, look on the bright side," Cassidy offers, taking in my beet red face. "At least you know you have options available." I can't control the laugh that escapes as she waggles her eyebrows at me.

"I'm not quite that desperate – yet. Okay, here's the deal. I like Ben a lot. Like a lot a lot. But, I don't want to like him. I want to bang him, scratch my little itch and then go back to my life where I'm at no risk of being hurt. I really don't think that's too much to ask for." My phone vibrates on the table but I ignore it as I await Cassidy's reply. I'm pretty sure I know what to expect, she's been fairly consistent in her disapproval of my attitude towards love all these years, but you never know, today might be the day she gets on board. But as I look across the table and into her bright blue eyes, I'm shocked by the sadness they hold.

"Babes, I love you. You are probably my favorite person in the entire world. You deserve to be so happy that I wanna puke at the amount of sun you're shining. Not every guy is going to hurt you, and even if they do, fuck them. You, babes, are a fucking warrior and you will survive it. You need to take chances though. Risk your heart a little bit. The payoff could be so incredible. You could find your person. And fifty years from now, when you're old and gray and your tits are hanging by your knees, are you really going to regret the chances you took? Or the ones that you let pass by?"

I feel the sting of tears as I process her words. Cassidy has experienced the devastation of heartbreak first hand and I know she's talking straight from the heart. The fact that she still opens herself up to the possibility of love makes her one of the most courageous people I know as far as I'm concerned, and I decide right here and now, to try to be as brave as she is.

"I promise not to act rashly, okay? I promise to give this a real chance and not just act out of fear. That's the best I can do."

Cassidy reaches over and squeezes my hand. "Well then, babes, that's all I expect from you."

Wyatt appears suddenly, plates in hand, and the air of gravity that had gripped us lifts. She slides our food along the table and plops herself down next to Cassidy.

"So, what are we talking about?" she enquires enthusiastically. My green eyes meet Cassidy's blue ones across the table and we reply in unison, "How 'bout them Mets?"

"Fuckers." She sighs as she reaches across and steals a piece of bacon from Cassidy's plate.

A few hours later, I am safely ensconced on my sofa, binge watching The Bachelor when I remember the missed text from earlier and pull my phone out to read it.

Ben: Last night was fun.
    Skye: It definitely was.
    Ben: It was hard saying goodbye, literally *wink*
    Skye: *groan*
    Skye: You didn't have to say goodbye.
    Ben: I was trying to be a gentleman.
    Ben: Don't worry, it won't happen again.
    Skye: Lol!
    Ben: I think, next time, I'd like to end the night with my face buried between your legs.

Oh, my holy shit. My face flames and my heart pounds at the image of Ben's head dipping between my thighs. Well, I did promise Cassidy I would give this a chance, right?

Skye: I'll look forward to that.

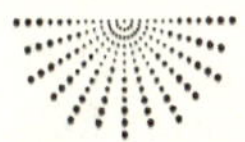

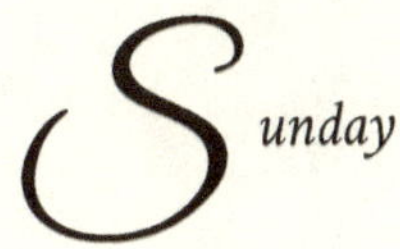unday

Ben: How adventurous are you?

Skye: Is this a sex question? Because you really need to work on your subtlety if it is.

Ben: LMAO. No, it's not a sex question.

Skye: Oh, then I guess I am reasonably adventurous. I'd like to think I'd give most things a go.

Ben: Great.

Ben: So, if it had been a sex question the answer would've been…

Skye: Pervert!

Monday

. . .

Ben: Are you afraid of heights?

Skye: No... why?

Ben: Because I'm going to take you to heaven, baby.

Skye: Oh my god *groans*

Ben: I'm making you cry for god and groan already? I'm better than I thought.

Skye: Yeah pretty sure I was groaning because that was one of the lamest things I've ever heard.

Ben: That's okay, when I'm using my tongue to explore every inch of your body, marking you with my teeth and finally tasting how sweet you are, I'm sure you won't think I'm so lame.

Skye: ….

Ben: No comeback?

Skye: Sorry my fingers were occupied.

Ben: Fuck.

Tuesday

Ben: I heard a song today and it had a line in it that made me think of you.

Skye: Oh yeah? What was the line?

Ben: I'd love to make you wet.

Skye: Aw you're such a romantic.

Ben: What could be more romantic than turning my girl on so much that she's dripping wet for me?

Skye: *blushes*

. . .

Wednesday

Skye: Thank you so much for the flowers!
　　Ben: Did you like them?
　　Skye: I love them so much, they're stunning!
　　Ben: Just like you.
　　Skye: Okay I think I may have just swooned a little lol.
　　Ben: Then my job here is done.

Thursday

Ben: So, what are your thoughts on hair pulling?
　　Ben: Because I can't get the idea of you on all fours, me pounding into you from behind with a handful of your hair in one fist and a tit in the other, out of my head.
　　Skye: I think I'd like that a lot.
　　Ben: Fuck, you want it rough?
　　Skye: I want it every way with you.
　　Ben: Oh, we are going to have some fun, baby.

Friday

Ben: Be ready at 11am, okay? And wear something comfortable that you can move around in.

Skye: Okay.
Ben: Also,
Skye: Yeah?
Ben: Wear black lace panties.

CHAPTER FIVE

*I*t's Saturday morning and I am scrambling to get ready for my date with Ben while my nerves beat a terrified drum in my chest. This past week we have messaged constantly, with our missives getting progressively more intimate, so I thought I knew what to expect today. Dinner and then a few hours being made dirty by this man whose mouth can make me wet with just a few simple words. But when he told me to be ready at 11am it threw me for a loop and I'm now feeling totally unprepared. Not to mention, a tad disappointed that I might not be getting to partake in the bedroom rodeo (ah Cassidy would be so proud) tonight.

The buzzer sounds, surprising me, and I let out a little squeak. Pressing the intercom, I tell Ben I'll be right down. As I gather all my gear I catch sight of the beautiful bouquet of pink roses and cherry blossoms that he sent me on Wednesday, sitting atop my small dining table. The exquisite mix of pink and white flowers are absolutely gorgeous and the sight of them immediately calms my nerves. Taking a deep breath, I close my eyes and take a few moments to center myself before moving toward the door.

Racing down the stairs, I burst through the door and am met by Ben, in all his glorious deliciousness, standing on the sidewalk. Looking casual in a pair of black basketball shorts and a gray sleeveless t-shirt with a pair of black sneakers on his feet, I'm tempted to call uncle and just beg him to take me upstairs so we can live out some of the fantasies we've talked about this week.

"You okay there, babe?" Ben questions, drawing my attention while my face flames in embarrassment at getting caught perving on this man.

I hastily reply with a quick, "Yep."

Leaning over and placing a gentle but firm kiss on my lips, Ben tells me that I look beautiful. Glancing down dismissively at my yoga pants and pink tank, I'm about to give a smartass reply when I glance up and see the heat in his eyes. Okay, maybe I might still get lucky today.

"So, where are we headed?" I ask. "You're being very enigmatic about today."

"You'll see, pipsqueak, let's walk." And with that, he takes off up the block, and I have to run to keep up with him.

"Pipsqueak?" I question as a memory lingers on the periphery of my consciousness, just out of reach. "Yeah that's not going to work for me," I say as I catch up to him.

"Have you seen you, Skye? You're fucking tiny. Plus, you make this little sound whenever my mouth gets anywhere near you. It kind of starts out as a squeak then turns into a gasp. Fucking sexy as hell."

Okay, so maybe pipsqueak will work for me.

As we walk toward destination unknown, we chat about random stuff, and I can't help but notice how easy this is. There have been no games from this man at all. Since day one he's been straightforward and upfront with me. I've never had to guess what he's thinking or if he's interested. I honestly didn't think men like this existed. My experience consisted of lying assholes who tried to manipulate me to get their own way. If I was going to fall for someone, it would be a guy like Ben. Now, I just need to find a way to resist him. Though, I have a feeling that will be easier said than done.

Twenty minutes later, we stop in front of a building that I don't recognize, which is odd since it's on my route to work; I must walk past it every day. It's a nondescript shop front with a sign proclaiming *Vertical Reality Climbing*, and I feel my jaw drop in horror.

"This is what you meant when you were asking if I was adventurous and afraid of heights?" I query.

"Yep. See, I wasn't being dirty at all. Maybe I'm not the only pervert here," he replies with a cheeky grin.

I'm quiet as I try to process what he's expecting me

to do, but apparently Ben takes this as acquiescence and, taking hold of my hand, pulls me inside.

As we enter, my fears are not allayed in any way. Immediately to our right is a huge room with three massive walls painted in a myriad of colors and containing what seems like thousands of tiny little things protruding from them. There's no way they are big enough for a hand to hold or a foot to stand on, and yet I fear that is indeed their purpose.

"I thought you were prepared to give anything a go?" Ben questions, and as he tries to contain his laughter I wonder if it's too soon in this relationship to punch him in the face.

Little does he know, I happen to have a stubborn streak as wide as the Grand Canyon, and he's just kicked it into gear.

"Let's go, baby cakes. Try to keep up with me, okay?" I throw over my shoulder as I make my way to the front desk.

A short while later we have completed the necessary paperwork and are standing in front of the beginner's wall (beginner's wall my ass, I think) in harnesses, while a very enthusiastic Kane ("but you can call me K-dog") walks us through the safety instructions and gives us an extensive list of do's and don'ts. My stomach is churning with nerves and for the first time in a month, they have nothing to do with the man standing beside me. But damned if I'll let him see how anxious I am.

"Are you sure you want to do this, Squeak?" I look up and see only sincerity in Ben's eyes. "Maybe this wasn't such a good idea. I kind of wanted to impress you, so I googled interesting date ideas and this seemed like a fun one. But now that I'm standing here, it seems like a very bad idea." I watch him as he makes this confession and my heart steps up a beat at the vulnerability he's allowing me to witness. He actually cared enough about this date to research it and he's now prepared to admit it may have been a mistake, just so I'm not forced to do something I don't want to. No way will I step all over his plans and make him feel like they are anything less than perfect.

"Are you kidding me? This is freaking awesome! Let's do this shit!" I gaze up at the wall and pray for the strength to pull this off.

"Oh my god, that was incredible! We have to do that again!" I am gushing as we leave the building an hour later. Sweaty and sore, nothing can thwart the high I'm feeling from the adrenaline coursing through my veins at this moment. I am completely exhilarated and ready to throw Ben down right here on the sidewalk and ride him like the grateful cowgirl I am. Instead, I throw myself into his arms and he catches me in a hug, squeezing me tight.

"So, you liked it then?" he responds with a laugh.

"Are you serious right now? What about you? How did you like it?"

"It was definitely a good workout. My arms are going to be killing me tomorrow, but it was a lot of fun. Although, I think I enjoyed hearing you whisper I think I can, I think I can, over and over again the most."

I'm pretty sure I die a little inside when I realize that he heard me repeat the mantra from my favorite children's book The Little Engine That Could, and I hide my face in his chest as he laughs at my embarrassment.

"Okay, next stop, lunch. Let's go." Ben takes hold of my hand, lacing his fingers with mine and we take off on foot.

"I'm not going to need to work out for the rest of the week after today, you're wearing me out," I say as my legs try to keep up with his much longer ones.

"Pace yourself, Squeak, we've still got the night to get through." He throws a sexy smirk my way as he pulls my hand up to his lush mouth and plants a kiss on it. And with that promise of what the night will bring, we continue our walk in comfortable silence. Once again, I am oblivious to our destination, but the subtle anticipation that Ben has provoked, combined with the intoxication that his scent evokes is keeping me in a state of bliss that renders me incapable of caring.

I'm so caught up in examining the notes of Ben's masculine smell, and trying to figure out why it's such a turn on, that I don't even notice the direction we are headed. Not until I look up and see that we are stopped in front of the beautiful leaf-embossed entrance to the Brooklyn Botanical Gardens. My heart drops. This place holds the most bittersweet memories for me. The last time I was here was the worst day of my life, until it was redeemed in the sweetest possible way.

Noticing that I've stopped in my tracks, Ben looks down at me, pulls me in close and says quietly, "This is one of my favorite places. Every time I come here, I'm reminded of a time that I had lost hope, and this is where, with a bit of help, I found it again. I wanted to bring you here because it's probably the most special place to me." With those simple words, I have never been so glad to be standing somewhere.

Reaching up on my tippy toes, I place a soft kiss on his lips. Ben steps closer, pulling me flush to his body and cupping the back of my head, his tongue lightly licks along the seam of my lips, seeking entrance. A slight groan escapes me and Ben is quick to take advantage. Slipping his tongue in my mouth, he deepens the kiss and my whole body alights with desire. Suddenly remembering where we are, I pull away and laugh lightly.

"You promised me food. Time to feed me, baby cakes."

He groans loudly at my use of this endearment. "So that's sticking, huh?"

Slapping a hand on his chest, I reply, "You get pipsqueak, I get baby cakes, it's your call."

Ben pauses, considering this, and finally retorts, "You know what? Baby cakes is suddenly growing on me. It makes me sound so masculine and virile, how could I not love it, Squeak?"

"Ugh, c'mon!" I drag him toward the ticket window. After getting our tickets, Ben leads the way inside and immediately heads toward Cherry Esplanade. As we approach, the memories assault me, however, I try my best to ignore them and stay in the moment, appreciating what Ben is sharing with me.

Coming to a stop he pulls his backpack off his shoulder, opens it up and pulls out a blanket. "This looks like the perfect spot, what do you think?" he asks.

"Perfect," I agree and as he smooths the blanket on the ground and pulls out some sandwiches from his bag, I muse out loud, "Well, you certainly came prepared."

He winks at me in a surprisingly non-douchey way and says, "You ain't seen nothing yet." Then with a flourish that would make a veteran game show hostess proud, he presents me with two Twinkies. I give him a slow clap and declare his moves very impressive. Laughing, he takes a bow before sitting down on the blanket and motioning for me to do the same.

Looking at the sandwiches, I place a hand on my heart and say, "Aw, did you cook for me, MacKinnon? You are such a catch."

"Hey, don't knock it. Not everyone can make a great PB&J, it requires skill and a steady hand. Luckily for you, I have both. And I'm not just talking about my sandwich making."

"Lame. You may need to work on your dirty talk as much as your cooking."

"Ouch." Ben clutches his chest. "You wound me. Thank god I have supreme confidence in my dirty-talking talents. For example, I know that tonight when I have my face buried between your thighs and I'm eating you out like you're my last meal, tongue fucking your delicious cunt, you're going to be completely satisfied with my skills."

My sandwich stops its path to my mouth and a sheen of sweat breaks out across my brow. Okay, yeah, the man's got mad skills, and I can't wait to experience them when I'm wearing considerably less clothing.

Deciding I need to change the subject if I want to make it through this afternoon with my panties intact, I ask him why these gardens are so meaningful to him. Ben's eyes lose focus slightly and I can almost feel the sadness rolling off him.

"When I was fifteen, my mom passed away, it was an intense time. Dad was struggling and it was incredibly hard to see him in so much pain. I was trying to cope with everything, but I was so angry. Angry at Mom for dying, angry at Dad for forgetting me in his own grief, and so fucking guilty for feeling that way. Then to top it all off, I found out we were moving; my father was taking us back to Connecticut where he grew up. He needed to be closer to his parents and sister, and I understood that. But at the time, it was the final straw. I felt like my entire world was collapsing. Then on my last day at school we came here on a field trip. I got paired up with this girl. We didn't know each other and I guess that made it easier to confide in her. I told her all the things that I felt too ashamed to admit to anyone else. Afterward she said to me—"

"You're allowed to be angry, but don't let your mother's death define you. Let her life inspire you." Ben's eyes widen as I repeat the words I said to him all those years ago.

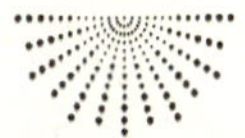

CHAPTER SIX

2 003

The chaotic sounds of teenagers echo around the school bus, but it's all white noise to me as I keep my gaze focused firmly out the window. I managed to snag a seat at the front of the bus so I could have it all to myself and I have diligently avoided my friends all morning. The last thing I feel like doing today is putting on a happy face and pretending it is a day like any other.

As my teacher, Ms. O'Brien, drones on about rules and expectations, I zone out again until my attention is abruptly drawn to the space next to me, where a boy I don't recognize has flopped down onto the seat. I glare at the side of his head, angry that he has burst my bubble of solitude, however, he keeps his eyes forward and ignores me. Well, two can play at that game. I go back to disregarding everyone and anything around me.

As the bus takes off I allow the movement to sooth my nerves and lull me into a semi-conscious state. I slept poorly last night, the tears flowing relentlessly as I replayed the words of my parents over and over, helpless to stop the pain they inflict. What feels like only minutes later, I am jostled awake by the bus coming to a stop in front of the Brooklyn Botanical Gardens, and I look up to find my seat mate staring at me. He looks slightly older than I am, with closely-cropped brown hair and a pair of wire-rimmed glasses covering his brown eyes, and I wonder how I've never seen him before and what he's doing on this field trip. I'm fairly certain he's not in any of the attending classes, but I don't get a chance to ask.

"You snore," he says quietly. Before I can respond, Ms. O'Brien is addressing the group.

"Okay, kids, you will be working in pairs today to complete your worksheets. Stay with the group and make sure you are always within sight of a teacher or chaperone. We have two hours and to make this easy your partner will be whoever you are sitting next to. Right, file out in an orderly fashion and collect your worksheet from Mr. Simmons."

My head is spinning. I can't believe I have to spend the next couple of hours playing nice with this stranger. He stands up and heads to the front of the bus and I reluctantly follow him. Five minutes later we have collected our paperwork and are standing at the entrance as students mill around laughing and shouting, enjoying themselves as if they don't have a care in the world. Meanwhile my broken heart has created an intense ache in my chest that I can't imagine ever going away.

"I'm Mack."

Looking up at my partner I try to give him a smile but I know it comes out more like a grimace. I also can't bring myself to care. "Skylah," I reply shortly.

"Well, Skylah, you look about as happy as I am to be here, so what do you say we get this over with as quickly as possible so we can go back to dwelling on our own misery like good teenagers should?"

For the first time in twenty-four hours I feel a small smile grace my lips. "That sounds like an excellent plan. Where do we start?"

"Let's head this way," he replies, pointing straight ahead. "I think the worksheet follows the path, so we should find everything we need pretty quickly." I nod my head in agreement. I'm all for getting this done as quick as possible.

We spend the next hour speeding through the worksheet while everyone else meanders all over the place, taking their time and enjoying their freedom from the confines of the school walls. Mack has proven to be a bit of a brainiac, and I have to admit, I'm curious as to why I've never seen him before.

We come upon Cherry Esplanade and in unspoken agreement we sit down under the beautiful blooming cherry blossom trees and fall into an easy silence. We're sitting right next to each other, so close that our hands are nearly touching and my heart picks up speed. Inwardly, I curse myself for this reaction. If last night taught me anything, it's that love and relationships are a waste of time and will only end in pain. While the last hour has been a distraction, my thoughts now return to the events of the previous night. So, in a desperate attempt to deflect my attention, I reach out to Mack, hoping that hearing about his silly overblown teenage angst will do the job.

"So, why are you so miserable then?" I ask.

Mack turns and looks me directly in the eye, assessing me, as if deciding whether I'm worthy of hearing his news. I have to suppress an eye roll. Please, as if I really care about whatever petty bullshit he has going on.

After pausing for a beat, Mack looks away and gazes up at the flowering branches above us.

"My mom died." And with those three words, my problems fade into insignificant oblivion.

My silence feels deafening as I run through a million things I could say, all the while knowing nothing could ever possibly help.

"You don't have to say anything. I know you're trying to think of the perfect thing, it's what everyone does. Then they spew some cliché bullshit and I have to pretend to be grateful. Silence is better." His eyes remain fixed upward, but from my position I can see the watery sheen they take on and my heart breaks a little for this boy who has lost more than even I could imagine.

"Do you want to talk about it? You're right, I have

no idea what to say, there's nothing I can say that will help, but I can listen."

He remains silent and I take that as my answer. I should probably get up and leave him alone, give him some space, but I just can't bring myself to leave him. So, I sit there and let the hum of the birds above soothe us.

"I'm so fucking angry. I know I shouldn't be, I should be sad and lost, but all I feel is anger." As Mack opens up I inch my pinky finger toward his and link them, offering him my support in the only way I know how.

"It was cancer. By the time they discovered it, it was stage four and terminal. She didn't even have a chance and she was gone six months later. I have no idea why I'm mad at her, but I am. I'm so mad she's gone; that she left me." Mack chokes up and I feel my own throat closing up in sympathy.

"My dad is completely lost. He just kind of wanders around, existing, doing his best to get through the day. At night I hear him cry, sobbing in his bedroom, and I want to help him somehow but I can't. Then I get angry at him too. Why is he hiding how upset he is? It makes me feel like I have to as well, like I can't let him know how out of control I feel. I'm trying to keep it together but I just…" as his voice trails off I glance over and see a tear escape.

"What was she like?" I ask.

"My mom? She was… amazing. Funny, so fucking funny. Compassionate. Kind. She treated everyone like family. She would have done anything for anyone." He lowers his head to his knees. "It's so fucking unfair."

"She sounds incredible."

His lips lift slightly at my remark. "She was the best."

Taking a deep breath, I consider my next words carefully. "You have every right to be angry, Mack. But don't let your mother's death define you. That would be the easy thing to do. Let her life inspire you. Live your life in a way that makes her memory shine." I shut my mouth and pray that I haven't overstepped. He lowers his head to his knees so I can no longer see his face, but his shoulders shake slightly and in an effort to offer him some sort of comfort I lean against him, placing my head against his arm and rubbing small circles on his back with my left hand.

We sit this way for what feels like an eternity until Mack has gathered himself. Looking across at me, he questions, "So, what happened to you, why are you so sad?"

I try to figure out how to answer him. After his revelations, my situation doesn't seem so important. Despite what happened last night, both my parents are alive and well. I can call either of them up and see them whenever I want. Honestly, I'm feeling like a drama queen right about now. I mean this is 2003, people's parents' divorce all the time, right?

"My parents told me last night that they're getting a divorce." I look at him almost apologetically and cringe at how unimportant that sounds after what he told me.

"Fuck. That sucks, I'm sorry." And his eyes tell me

that he is sorry. That despite everything he's going through, he has the empathy to feel badly for me. The thought crosses my mind that he's more like his mother than he thinks he is.

"Yeah. I had no clue they were unhappy, it was just the way they were. Which is really sad if you think about it. They must have been miserable for so long that it was the only way I knew them to be." I sigh as I consider this for the millionth time. How is it possible to not know your parents were that unhappy? Was I that selfish?

"How did it go down? Was there yelling and fighting?" Mack asks.

"No, not really. I mean, there was no fighting, but it was obvious there was something wrong. Mom was drinking and just seemed really angry. Dad was…" Tears well up as I recall my father's demeanour last night. "He was happy, like he seemed relieved to be getting it all out, he was happy to be leaving us. Anyway, he explained that him and Mom hadn't been happy and that he had met someone else. He didn't mean for anything to happen, but he fell in love and he was leaving to be with her. He seriously couldn't even pretend to be sad. Even when I cried, he just said that it would all work out for the best, I would see. And then he left. He just walked out while I stood at the door watching him walk away."

"Well aren't we just a motherfucking perfect pair, huh?" Mack asks and I snuffle out a laugh through the tears that had started to fall.

"Yep, we definitely are."

"You know what? I'm sorry you went through that, but can I tell you something?" As I nod my head, he continues, "Don't let that change your opinion on love. Because real love is amazing. My parents were so in love with each other, it used to gross me out." A smile breaks out across his cute face. "They were forever making out and holding hands. I mean yeah, they fought, but I remember Mom telling me once that fighting in a relationship could be a great thing. That it meant they trusted each other and their relationship enough to disagree and to have that kind of trust in someone was magic. So, it might not always work out, but love is real and it can be fucking incredible."

I smile broadly at his declaration. "How have we never met before?" I finally ask the question that has been plaguing me all afternoon.

"I'm a sophomore, not a freshman. My English class is on a field trip right now to see the local community theater performance of a play that's about a dying mother. The guidance counsellor said if I didn't feel up to going to the play then I could come on this field trip instead. We did this last year, so I figured it would be an easy way to pass an afternoon."

"Well, I'm glad you did. It's probably really selfish of me, but you made me feel a lot better, so thank you."

"Yeah, you actually made some sense too, pipsqueak," he replied, gently nudging my shoulder with a laugh.

"Pipsqueak? Yeah that won't work for me. Do I need to pull out the four-eyes jokes?" I retort.

"Whatever, these glasses add to my sex appeal," he

replies and I groan loudly at this, coughing out "lame" into my hand. It feels good to laugh and I hope Mack feels the same way. I'm trying to work up the nerve to somehow ask him if he'd be interested in going out sometime. It would be nice to have someone to talk to about all of this, someone who understands. At least, that's what I'm telling myself. It has nothing to do with big brown eyes and how they crinkle when his beautiful smile lights up his face. No, that would be ridiculous. Mack interrupts my thoughts before I get a chance.

"Today's my last day. Dad is moving us back to Connecticut where he grew up. He wants to be closer to his parents and sister."

"Oh." That's honestly the only response I can come up with.

"I mean, I understand it. Doesn't mean I'm happy about it. I hate that I have to leave my friends, my school. Especially my home. There's so many good memories there, you know?"

"Yeah, that must be really tough."

"I just wanted you to know, because if I wasn't leaving I would have asked you out. I just thought you should know that."

A short distance away, Ms. O'Brien calls out to all the kids, trying to rally them all back to the school bus.

"Well, Mack, I would have said yes. Just so you know." And with that I begin to gather my belongings.

"Skylah?" I look over and suddenly his lips are brushing across mine in the sweetest kiss I could have imagined. It tastes like hope and might-have-beens.

Mack breaks the kiss and gives me a smile that repairs a tiny piece of my shattered heart. Then he gets up, throws his backpack over his shoulder and holds out his hand to me. In that moment, right there under those cherry blossoms, my faith in the possibility of love is restored.

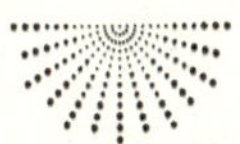

CHAPTER SEVEN

"*How* the fuck is that possible?" Ben asks incredulously. He reaches up and gently tugs on a lock of hair. "Your hair was darker then," he says softly. "And shorter. How could I not recognize you though? That day was such a huge deal for me."

"I also had braces. You had glasses and were about four inches shorter. It was fifteen years ago, we grew up. Matured. We don't look the same as we did back then. Why would we even think it would be a possibility? I never thought I would see you again."

"This is unbelievable. I can't believe it's actually you." And before I know what's happening, his lips are on mine, aggressively taking what he needs from me. I melt into him, happy that I'm able to give him this and fully prepared to give him anything else he wants.

"My place," I mutter as his mouth briefly leaves mine. "Now."

I attempt to slot my key into the lock, but as I feel the heat of Ben's body right behind me, I only seem to be capable of fumbling it. He takes a step closer, his body now completely covering my own as he pushes me into the door. Grabbing my ass, he grinds his cock into me and my breath hitches. Running his lips along my neck, he gently bites down, and my pussy pulses in anticipation. Covering my hand with his own, he brings the key up to the lock and slides it in. I'm about to make a joke about how well he fills my hole when we are suddenly falling through the now-open doorway, immediately a tangle of limbs as our hands explore every inch they can. His hard body feels incredible to my touch and the strength he exudes is overwhelming. The late afternoon light casts a soft glow over the room and as Ben moves me forward, his mouth never leaves mine, devouring me, and all I can think is how good he tastes.

With a small grunt, he breaks our kiss and utters one word. "Bedroom?"

I point in the direction of my room, and as he picks me up, my legs wrap instinctively around his waist and my mouth finds his neck, kissing up toward his jaw and enjoying the sensation of his scruff against my lips.

Reaching the bed, he throws me down and gives me a small smirk as he watches me bounce.

"Get rid of the clothes." With that firm directive, he begins removing his own. My eyes are glued to him as his body is quickly revealed to me. His broad, muscled chest is giving me serious heart eyes, but as my eyes move downward, it's the sight of that delicious V and the happy trail leading to what I imagine will be my very happy place, that has me salivating. His hands suddenly still and I almost cry out in disappointment as they leave the waistband of his shorts, leaving me frustrated that the big reveal has been delayed.

He grabs my ankles and with a sharp yank, pulls me down to the end of the bed. He leans down until his chest covers mine and his face is only inches from my own. "I said clothes off."

As his breath ghosts over my lips I feel his hands slide under the waistband of my yoga pants and move downwards, removing them while he caresses his way down my legs. My heart is thumping as he straightens and stares down at me, looking as though he is about to do all the dirty things to me.

"You wore the black panties." He doesn't sound at all surprised that I followed his instructions and it makes me want to challenge him.

"It's laundry day, they were all I had left." He laughs at my obvious lie.

"Whatever you need to tell yourself, Squeak. Move up the bed." Again, I want to challenge him. But I also want him to fuck me and it turns out my desire for that is stronger than my stubbornness, so I do as he commands, moving up the bed until my head rests on the pillow.

Finally, he removes his shorts, and taking his boxer briefs right along with them, I am left with an unob-structed view of what might possibly be one of the most beautiful cocks I have ever seen. Long and thick with a single vein running along the top of the shaft, it is practically calling out to be swallowed up. A hand wraps around what was to be my next meal, and Ben fists his cock a couple of times before crawling up the bed. His body hovers over mine, his eyes taking in every inch of me, and while I should feel self-conscious, the heat in his gaze leaves me feeling nothing but wanted. As he continues up, he drags my tank top with him, removing it easily and leaving me exposed in only my bra and panties. Whispering a kiss across my lips, I'm left wondering how the smallest touch from him leaves me dripping wet.

"So. Fucking. Beautiful." His words bring my attention right back where it belongs, and as he moves slowly down my body, his tongue tracing a sensual path, I feel the anticipation build.

He makes quick work of removing my panties, and as he looks up at me from under his lashes, his eyes hold a promise of delicious wickedness. Leaning down he places gentle kisses along my thigh. That, combined with his stubble scratching my soft skin, creates a riot of sensation. After what feels like a lifetime, he finally reaches my aching pussy, and I gasp quietly as he nudges me with his nose and inhales deeply. Grunting out something unintelligible, he pushes his face into my cunt and I just about lose my mind. He licks me slowly, and reaching my swollen clit, he flicks it a few times before lightly biting down. I'm so turned on by this guy that I could almost come from that alone. Ben is relentless as he slides two fingers inside me. Crooking them, he finds that sweet spot that almost has me vaulting off the bed.

"So fucking good, Squeak, your pussy tastes so sweet." And then his mouth is back on me, finishing what it started. His tongue and fingers move in tandem, overwhelming me, and I can't stop my hands from tugging on his hair and pulling his face closer as I grind my pussy against it.

"Fuck, oh my god, fucking yes, that's, oh my god, fuuuuuck!" With a final, firm suck of my clit, Ben has me coming so hard I think I may very well black out for a few seconds.

Lifting his head, he licks his lips and gives me a self-satisfied smile. Rising to his knees, he reaches back for his shorts and fumbles for a minute before producing a condom. Rolling it along his length, he bends down and kisses me. His tongue invades my mouth and I can taste the sweetness of myself.

"Are you on the pill?" he asks, and apparently, I am still in an orgasm-induced fog, so all I can do is nod.

"Good, now I'm going to fuck your tight little cunt and see if it feels as unbelievable as it tastes." He grasps his dick and teases it over my already over-sensitized clit. Just as I'm about to beg him to stop, he pulls back and lines himself up with my entrance. Looking me straight in the eye, he slams into me, filling me completely. Stilling himself, he gives me some time to acclimate to his size and lightly caresses my cheek. "I'm so glad I found you."

I feel my eyes sting with unshed tears at his words.

As he begins to thrust, slowly moving in and out of me, he kisses his way down my neck and his mouth finds my breast. He tongues my nipple with the same intensity he showed my pussy and then, using his teeth, he bites down roughly; the sting intensifying everything. All the while his hand palms my other breast, squeezing, pinching, groping. Every little move adding to the myriad of sensations that are making me lose control. His hot mouth is all over me, his tongue licking and tasting. He grunts softly as if he can't control himself, and oh my god that does something to me.

Straightening up, he rises to his knees. Maintaining a firm grip on my hips, he pulls me right along with him, and I watch him as his eyes remain glued to where he is entering me.

"Fuck, look at that, babe. Watch how your pussy takes my dick like they were fucking made for each other." My eyes immediately drop and he's right. The sight of him sliding into me, covered in my arousal makes the pulsing in my cunt intensify, and as his thumb finds my clit, I feel my orgasm hit me in a violent wave that leaves me screaming out his name.

Ben's rhythm falters, his thrusts becoming faster, his grunts louder. His grip on my hips borders on painful, but I love the thought of seeing his mark on me tomorrow. As he pounds into me I notice the sheen of sweat covering his body and see him lose his final shred of control. With a loud, "Fuck," he comes, pushing himself into me as deep as he can get; I feel him throbbing inside me.

Placing my ass back down on the bed, he lies down over me and puts his head on my breasts. Breathing hard, I can feel his smile against my skin, and before his beautiful cock has even left the warmth of my pussy, I have decided that we are definitely doing that again.

❦

Lying in a messy bed on a Saturday evening, luxuriating under the feeling of Ben's fingers trailing up and down my arm, I could possibly be the happiest I've ever been.

"What happened after?" Ben's voice breaks through my thoughts.

"After?"

"After that day, what happened with your mom and dad?"

"Oh." I feel that familiar uncomfortable tug in my chest that I get when I think about my parents.

"I barely saw my dad after that. He eventually married the chick he cheated on Mom with. She had a little girl, Danielle, who was only four, I think, when they got married. They kind of became their own little unit and it never really felt right for me to be there. Mom moved on, but she was pretty bitter about what happened. She never met anyone else and pretty much retreated into herself. By the time I graduated high school she was a fairly absent parent. She worked around the clock and that seemed to be the only thing that brought her any kind of happiness. I started working at Books & Beans when I was eighteen and Juliet became like a surrogate mother to me. Then I met Cassidy when I started college and they've basically been my family ever since."

He pulls back slightly so he can meet my eyes, he seems to be searching for something.

"I'm sorry. I'm really sorry that was how your story went. Any time I thought about that girl under the cherry blossoms, I always hoped her parents had worked things out. I wanted you to be okay." The sincerity in his voice almost breaks me, but I swallow down the lump in my throat and hold his gaze.

"I'm good, really. Do I wish things had worked out differently? Sometimes. But I'm pretty happy with my life, so I won't complain. What about you? How did things play out with your dad?"

"Really well, actually. I think moving back to Connecticut helped him, having that family support. My aunt convinced him to get some counselling to help him grieve, then he convinced me to go too. I was able to work through all that anger that was festering and we got to a really good place. Dad even met someone a few years ago and they got married last year. That caused a few tricky moments for both of us. He felt guilty for falling in love again and I definitely struggled a bit seeing him with another woman. She's great though, Fiona, and she really loves my dad so we made it work. We were very lucky."

A contented sigh escapes me and I think how lucky we both have been to find each other again. Turning over, I roll on top of him and pop a chaste kiss on his lips.

"Wanna get lucky again?"

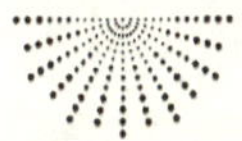

CHAPTER EIGHT

Skye: Sooooooo….

Ben: Soooooo?

Skye: Cassidy is insisting on meeting you.

Ben: The infamous Cassidy. I don't know whether to be excited or terrified.

Skye: Terrified. The answer is terrified.

"Stop that!"

Tap, tap, tap, tap.

I glare at Cassidy as she continues to tap her nails on the table top.

"Can you please stop, you're driving me insane."

"He's not coming, is he? Spanky's standing me up."

"Like I've told you about thirty times in the last twenty minutes, he is coming, he messaged me and he's just running a bit late, that's all. And oh my god he has a name, Cass, please use it when he gets here, I beg you."

Cassidy rolls her eyes and my frustration mounts. "I'm not making any promises. I'm going to use the bathroom, be right back." As she sashays away, I bury my head in my arms and suppress a loud groan. This has disaster written all over it. Cassidy and Ben are both way too eager to meet each other, and the butterflies in my stomach are telling me that there's a train wreck ahead.

Sucking in a deep, calming breath, I raise my head to indulge in some people watching; one of my guilty pleasures. The restaurant is a bustling hive of activity, and my eye is immediately drawn to what appears to be a father and his young daughter a few tables down. They are sitting across from each other and the girl's eyes shine with delight as her father lavishes attention on her. The little girl appears to be telling him a story and he is as enthralled as I find myself to be. He listens in rapt silence and as I examine his face I feel a small tug of jealousy that I never got to experience this with my father. He was never around much when I was little, preferring to work or be with his friends watching a game and drinking. And then he was gone.

A hand grasps my shoulder, giving it a small squeeze and startling me out of my melancholy. I almost jump out of my seat and look up to see Ben watching me intently.

"You okay, Squeak? You were in another world there."

The smile that always follows Ben's appearance

lights up my face. "I'm good, just got a bit lost in my head for a second, that's all."

He sits down in the chair next to mine, leans over and places a soft kiss behind my left ear, his lips leaving a trail of goosebumps behind.

"You look gorgeous, babe." I feel my face heat at his compliment and offer him thanks.

"I might need to fuck you in the bathroom at some point tonight."

"Well, aren't you just a fucking pervert then." Cassidy plonks herself down, sitting on the other side of me with her attention fixed solely on Ben. "Nice of you to join us, Tarzan."

Ben looks quizzically between the two of us and all I can do is shrug. I have no idea what is going on in that head of hers, and honestly, I think it's probably safer not to know. Ben, however, doesn't know her well enough to realize this.

"Tarzan?" he queries.

"Skyballs told me how you call out like Tarzan when you come. You know, ah-ah-ah-ah!" She does her very best Tarzan impression until I slap my hand over her mouth to shut her up. Ben's eyes are as wide as saucers and I have no clue how this is going to play out.

Finally, a loud laugh escapes him and I sigh in relief before turning my attention to my possibly ex best friend.

"I did not say that, Cassidy Jensen, you dirty little liar!" And then there were two. My head swings rapidly back and forth between the two of them as Cassidy joins Ben in his laughter and they seemingly take great joy in my discomfort.

"I knew I was going to like you, Cassidy," Ben says when they finally manage to calm themselves. "But I have the distinct feeling I may need some alcohol tonight, so how about we order?"

"You're a man after my own heart, Benjamin," Cassidy replies and then turning to me she says in a mock whisper, "See, I can use his name." She pokes her tongue out at me.

I sigh. It's going to be a long night.

Four hours later, all my fears have proved to be unfounded as the three of us sit around the table laughing uncontrollably as Ben tells the story of how he and his friend Mason ended up thrown out into the street, in only their boxer briefs, after a game of strip poker went horribly wrong in college.

"Oh my god, that's gold!" I exclaim as I try to tamp down my giggles, but every time I try I imagine Ben lying on the pavement in only his underwear and beautiful smile, and more laughter escapes. Turning my head, I catch Ben staring at me. No longer laughing, a small smile is playing at his lips and his eyes are filled with an emotion I'm too scared to identify.

"What?" I ask softly.

"You're just really beautiful, you know that?" He reaches over, tucks my hair behind my ear and pulls me firmly to him, kissing me gently. Just as he pulls me closer and starts to deepen the kiss, a cough interrupts us.

"Gag me, guys," Cassidy says, pulling a face. "Although, I suppose I should be grateful you were able to prevent yourselves from the public fucking you were promising earlier."

"The night's not over yet, I may just drag Squeak away yet."

"Okay, explain the Squeak thing, it's so cute it's cringeworthy." After examining me in a way that makes me super uncomfortable, she continues, "It suits her though."

"I don't know whether to be flattered or insulted," I throw right back at her.

"Yeah, don't look too closely at it, Skyballs."

Chuckling to himself as he watches our back and forth, Ben answers her question simply and with a shrug. "She's a pipsqueak. Your turn. The Skyballs thing. Explain."

"Well, your girl here has a real issue with eyeballs. They completely freak her out. Did you ever see that episode of Friends?" He shakes his head no and she continues, "Well, you should watch it. Skye is a complete Rachel and it amuses the hell out of me. And that, my friend, is how Skyballs was born."

We continue to sit and laugh for another hour or so and I could not be more thrilled with how tonight is going. Ben and Cassidy have instinctively fallen into an almost quasi sibling relationship and it triggers a visceral reaction in me. Cassidy is essentially my family, the most important person in the world to me, and seeing the two of them like this opens my heart up to Ben even further.

As we settle the check and prepare to leave, Cassidy throws her arms around Ben in a full-on bear hug, almost knocking him off his feet. After a brief moment of surprise, he wraps his arms around her and squeezes her tight.

"I like you, Ben. But, I love her. So, trust me when I say, if you hurt her I'll cut your dick off and use it for my own very special brand of turkey slap."

"Noted," he says, smiling into the top of her head.

I feel the sting of tears at this exchange until I notice her hands snake down to Ben's delectable ass and give it a squeeze.

"Get your hands off my man's ass, Jensen."

"I'm only human, Balls, and that ass? Bravo, Ben."

As I sit in the back seat of the car on the way back to my apartment, curled into Ben's side and enjoying the warmth of his body, I consider all the things his dirty mouth is going to do to me in the not too distant future, when my phone dings. Pulling it out I see Cassidy's name on the screen.

Cassidy: He'll do.

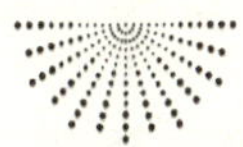

"Pass me one of those sugar cookies, Skylah, I can't resist them any longer." I smile at Juliet's request and, using the tongs in the jar, I remove the biggest cookie and place it on a napkin for her.

Taking the treat with a smile, Juliet continues, "I'm so proud of you, my love. My accountant told me that the last month has been the shop's most successful in the last two years. Those changes you implemented have certainly worked." My smile widens at her words. I had been nervous about making changes to what had been a winning formula, but the risk had paid off and we had seen an increase in our profits over the last month.

"Thank you, J, that means a lot. I still have a few more ideas that I'm working on, but I don't want to make too many changes too quickly."

"Absolutely. Now, enough business talk, tell me how things are going with your young man." Upon hearing

Juliet's question, Layla suddenly appears in front of us, plops herself down on a stool in front of the counter, places her chin in her hands and looks at me expectantly. Juliet chuckles while I roll my eyes.

"You know, it's so easy to forget that you're related to Cassidy. Until you pull shit like that, Lay."

She shrugs and widens her eyes innocently.

"Us Jensen's like the gossip, what can I say? Now spill!"

I try to present an air of nonchalance, but on the inside, I'm a giddy child. These last few months with Ben have been incredible. Since that day at the Botanical Gardens, things have progressed with a speed and intensity that I never would have imagined I would love. Every day I fall a little harder. The man has the kindest heart and he makes me laugh like no one else. Ben makes me feel safe and it would be so easy to become consumed by him. And for the first time, the thought of that doesn't terrify me. I have, however, tried to temper my enthusiasm when it was pointed out to me that I may be talking about him a little too often. "It's going so well, I'm really happy. He makes me happy," I answer simply.

"I'm so pleased to hear that, Skylah. It's about time you allowed yourself to be swept away by some debonair gentleman."

"From what I hear, he's not much of a gentleman, if you know what I mean." Layla waggles her eyebrows at us.

"Layla, that's enough of that!" Juliet chastises before

following with, "We need some wine if we're going to go there." She throws a wink my way with a sly smile.

Then as if all our talk has conjured him up, the bell to the front door jingles and Ben walks through. As he looks around the shop I take this moment to appreciate his physicality before he notices me. Tall and broad, he dwarfs me in every direction, and I adore the sense of security that gives me when I am with him. His face is beautiful, in a completely masculine sense. Dark brown eyes, that remind me of melted chocolate, are filled with mischief more often than not. The imperfection of a slight bump on his nose only adds to his appeal, and a strong jaw, that is usually covered in a slight scruff, has my thighs clenching anytime I stare too long. His huge smile has the ability to light up his entire face, which is exactly what is happening now as he spots me from his position in the doorway.

Moving quickly, his long legs eat up the space between us in no time, and he stops right in front of me. I can feel a grin on my face that matches his in size and brightness.

"Hi," I whisper.

"Hey, Squeak." He leans down and, cupping my face in both hands, he places a soft kiss on my mouth that makes my every pulse point jump.

Breaking our kiss before it has a chance to really begin, Ben looks over at Juliet and Layla who are almost swooning where they stand. Reaching out to shake their hands, he introduces himself. Layla, her face a bright shade of red, briefly takes his hand before rushing off to finish shelving the new arrivals. I sigh as I watch her go. That girl is as shy as Cassidy is outrageous, and I really do worry about her sometimes.

Turning my attention back to Ben and Juliet, I see them quietly conversing as if they've known each other forever. It's a wonderful skill Ben has, the ability to put people at ease immediately, and one that I admire greatly.

Wrapping my arm around his waist, I give a squeeze as I listen to Juliet telling Ben about her retirement, and I bask in the peace this moment fills me with. When there is a lull in the conversation I turn to Ben and ask what he's doing here.

"I was able to finish work early, so I thought I'd swing by and surprise you. Maybe hang around and watch you be all bossy until closing time and then take you out to dinner," he replies.

"That sounds like an awesome plan. I am feeling particularly bossy today, so you lucked out." I laugh.

"Skylah, you two head out now. Layla and I can close up, it's only a half an hour anyway, off you go," Juliet says.

"J, I can't ask you to do that. He can wait, can't you, baby cakes?" I throw at Ben.

"Of course, I can."

"Nonsense, I won't hear any arguing. Off you go." She shoos us away like we're an annoying bug.

Ben and I look at each other and I shrug. "Well, if she insists, there's no point arguing."

"Exactly," Juliet replies as she reaches down under

the counter and hands me my purse and jacket. Taking them from her, I give her a kiss and thank her.

"Have a wonderful night, my love." My heart swells from the look in her eyes. I miss seeing her every day, and today's visit has reminded me exactly how much. Before my mood dampens, I take Ben's hand and head for the doorway, calling out goodbye to Layla on our way. On the other side of the door, Ben drapes his arm over my shoulders.

"I know a great little restaurant not far from here, how do you feel about Italian?" Ben asks.

"Um I feel like I would kiss your special place for a good lasagna right now."

"My special place?" Ben guffaws at my attempt to be discreet. "Are you offering to suck my dick in exchange for Italian food, Squeak? Because if that's the case I can get you lasagna every damn day."

"Oh my god." Laughing, I turn and hide my face in his shoulder. "Just feed me."

"I'm trying." Ben laughs.

"Food, Mackinnon. Feed me food!" And with that, Ben grabs my hand and practically drags me to the restaurant.

Later, as we sit chatting over coffee after enjoying a delicious meal, Ben's attention is drawn to the register where a tall man with tousled light brown hair and an expensive-looking suit is staring solemnly at his phone.

"Mason!" Ben calls out, and the man looks over and smiles when he sees Ben motioning for him to join us.

As Mason ambles over to us, Ben throws me an apologetic glance.

"You don't mind, do you?"

"Of course not! It's about time I got to meet him."

"Yeah, he's been working crazy fucking hours lately. I'm kind of glad to see him out of the office."

Mason arrives and Ben stands up and pulls him into a hug with a firm back slap.

"Hey, man, it's good to see you. Have a seat and meet my girl," Ben says, pointing at a spare chair at our table and sitting down.

"Mason this is Skye. Skye, Mason." Mason reaches across the table to shake my hand.

"Skye, great to finally meet you. I'm sorry it hasn't happened sooner, work's been kicking my ass lately. But rest assured I've heard all about you by text. Ben's been gushing like a pre-teen girl talking about Bieber." Mason's last statement causes me to laugh out loud.

"Well, I'm glad to meet you too, Mason, I've heard a lot of stories about you, that's for sure, so it's nice to put a face to the name."

Mason groans in response. "None of it's true, I swear."

"So, you didn't strip Ben naked and leave him lying under a tree on campus once? I've got to say I'm disappointed," I challenge him.

"Oh, well that's absolutely true. But in my defence, he was drunk and getting handsy with me. And I did leave him a pillow, so I think I'm the good guy in that story."

"The good guy, seriously dude?" Ben interrupts. "I woke up surrounded by a bunch of people laughing and taking photos of my junk; which was definitely not at its best considering how freezing it was. That shit could've scarred me and my dick for life."

"I will admit that I may have been slightly inebriated myself, so my judgement wasn't the best. But if I recall, the pictures didn't hurt your manwhore status at all, in fact they may have even helped," Mason swiftly retorts.

"Manwhore, huh?" I question. "Now this he never mentioned." Mason laughs at this.

"Doesn't surprise me. Until the Amber incident, Ben was legendary on campus." My eyes widen slightly at this statement and seek out Ben's. He has vaguely mentioned in passing about a messy romantic history, but hadn't gone into specifics and I didn't want to push him. The air is thick with tension. Mason, realizing that he may have put his foot in his mouth, looks around the restaurant awkwardly, and Ben refuses to make eye contact with me. Thank goodness Mason's food arrives at that moment and he makes a hasty retreat.

"It was great meeting you, Skye. I'm sorry if I fucked up just now. That's all in Ben's past, he's a different man now, and he really cares about you. Don't listen to a word I say, okay?"

"It's fine, Mason, please don't worry about it; I'm

not." I stand and give him a brief hug to show there are no hard feelings.

"You don't have to leave, Mase, it's fine. Stay and eat with us, we were planning on another coffee, right, Squeak?"

"I definitely won't say no to another," I reply.

"Thanks, but I can't, I have to get back to the office."

"It's Friday night, man, you can't take the night off?" Ben asks.

"No, we're trying to push a deal through at the moment so everyone's working around the clock to meet deadlines. Things should settle down in the next few weeks though, maybe we could all have dinner then?"

"Sounds like a plan, make it happen, okay?" Ben stands, slaps Mason on the back and returns to his seat.

"It was nice to meet you, Mason, I'll look forward to that dinner." He returns my smile before turning and walking out of the restaurant.

"So, manwhore, huh?" I say with a smile.

"He's exaggerating," he scoffs.

"Uh huh, I'm sure." I roll my eyes at him. "Can I ask what the Amber situation was?"

Ben sighs and takes a large sip of his coffee.

"Amber was my ex-girlfriend. Or ex fiancée, I should say."

The teaspoon I am holding clatters to the table as I try to process what he just told me.

"Okay. Ex fiancée. That feels like maybe something you should have mentioned before now."

"I know, Skye, and I'm sorry. I've been trying to tell

you for ages but it's hard for me to talk about. That was a really bad time in my life and I hate thinking about it."

"I understand. But I do need to know." I stand firm in my resolve. If we're to continue with this relationship he is going to have to be honest.

"I know. You deserve to know." He leans back in his seat, takes my hand and holding it tight, places it on his lap.

"Okay, so Mason wasn't lying. I was a bit of a manwhore back then. It was my first time away from home, I was enjoying my freedom and I didn't want to be tied down. I dated a lot. I fucked a lot. I had a lot of fun. Then one day, this girl I had dated casually, Amber, came to me and told me she was pregnant. I freaked out. I totally lost it for a while there. Mason got my dad to come down and he pretty much talked me off the ledge. Told me I had to man up. If I was going to go out dicking around I had to be prepared to deal with the consequences, and he was right. So, I got my head straight, accepted this was happening and actually started to get pretty excited about it. Then Amber told me that her parents were pissed as hell and threatening to cut her off and not pay for college unless she got married. That they couldn't face the shame of their unmarried daughter having a baby." He shakes his head at the memory, and takes a deep breath before continuing.

"It didn't make much sense. I mean it was two thousand and fucking ten, you know? Nobody cares about shit like that. But she was devastated and I felt awful. I figured we could get engaged, say we were having a long engagement and then once she finished college, break it off. We were both about to start our last year so that seemed logical. Initially she agreed but then she started putting the pressure on. Saying her parents weren't okay with that and they weren't going to pay her last year's tuition unless we got married before the year started. And Amber was so persuasive. She convinced me we could make it work. That we could take a shot at being a proper family, for the sake of our baby. So, I agreed and we made plans for a simple elopement to Vegas. Because that's how all great love stories start, right?" He snorts. I squeeze his hand to encourage him to continue.

"Anyway, the day we were supposed to leave, Amber's friend Jo came and saw me. It turns out that none of it was true. Amber wasn't pregnant at all. She had just set her sights on me, convinced herself that she loved me. Which was ridiculous, she barely knew me. When I confronted her about it she broke down and confessed it all. She said she was sorry but she just loved me so much and couldn't bear the idea of not having me. I was sickened." He squeezes his eyes shut tight, as if trying to protect himself from the memories.

"I had fallen in love with that baby. I was so goddamn excited by that point and finding out that it didn't exist just about killed me. I swore off women for the longest time. I threw myself into school and gradu-ated with honors. Then threw myself into my work. I've dated a little bit over the last few years but I found it hard to trust women, so relationships ended pretty quickly." Bringing my hand up to his mouth he brushes a kiss across it and turns to look at me.

"And then there was you."

"And then there was me," I whisper.

Right then and there, the last tiny bit of my wall crumbles and the truth crashes down on me.

I'm in love with this man.

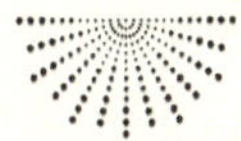

CHAPTER TEN

Stepping out of the shower, I reach for the towel and begin to dry my hair. I'm excited for girls' night tonight and eager to have some time with Cassidy and Wyatt. Since my revelation last week concerning my feelings for Ben, I've been feeling off kilter, my emotions all over the place. What I really need right now is Cassidy to kick my ass and Wyatt to smother me in love. I need my girls.

After drying off, I wrap myself in a pink towel, walk out of the bathroom and into my bedroom where I find Ben lying on my bed in only a pair of basketball shorts, scrolling through his phone. My heart does this weird little palpitating thing at the sight of his broad, bare chest. I love how at ease he is in my home. It makes it incredibly easy to envision this as our home. A thought that calms the chaos swirling through my head.

Ben's eyes immediately seek me out and I can feel the weight of his stare as I approach the mirror on my dresser and prepare to put my face on.

"What are you doing tonight?" I ask him as I reach for my moisturizer and begin to apply it. When no answer is forthcoming I turn to face him, and see his eyes burning into me with an intensity I haven't seen before. I can feel the blush spread across my face under the heat of his scrutiny and I look away, feeling self-conscious.

"You're so fucking sexy, Skye." He bounds across the room and stands behind me. Turning my body so that I am facing him, he leans down and places his forehead gently against mine. Closing his eyes, he inhales deeply, breathing me in.

I've never experienced this before. The physical connection between us is visceral and intoxicating. It completely overwhelms me and I find myself wanting to experience everything with him.

Brushing my mouth across his jaw, a low moan escapes him as his stubble chafes my lips in a most delicious way. I continue my path downward, kissing and licking, nibbling and tasting until my knees hit the carpeted floor and I look up at Ben from beneath my lashes.

He brushes his knuckles softly across my cheek and I lean forward, placing an open-mouthed kiss below his belly button.

Reaching up, I take hold of his waistband and pull his shorts and boxers down, tormenting us both with the slowness of my movements.

His cock is at the perfect height, pointing right at my mouth, and who am I to ignore what's right in front of me?

Leaning forward, I lick the tiny bead of pre-cum glistening on the tip and follow it with a ghost of a kiss. Ben sucks in a ragged breath and that simple sound fills me with all the confidence I need. Opening my mouth, I take him in slowly and a groan escapes me as the taste of him hits my taste buds. Reaching down, Ben undoes my towel, watching it drop and exposing my body to him, his eyes close and squeeze shut as though he is trying to gain control of himself. Then threading his right hand through my long hair, he grabs a handful and uses it to guide my mouth along his shaft. I go willingly, enjoying the feel of his dominance. Pressing forward until I begin to gag, I pull back slightly and then swallow, relishing the strangled sound Ben makes at the sensation of my throat tightening around his cock.

"Baby?" Ben chokes out and I look up at him, my mouth full of his dick. "Do you trust me?" Without hesitating, I nod yes. Ben pulls out so only the crown of his cock is sitting on my lips.

"I'm going to fuck your mouth now, Squeak, so open wide, babe." He holds tight to my head with both hands and begins thrusting. Slow and steady to begin with, he quickly loses the battle to stay in control. Slamming into my mouth, the noises coming out of him are driving me crazy. I'm gagging on every thrust, but I love that I have the power to unravel this man.

"Look at me," Ben harshly whispers and my watery eyes meet his. I can see every bit of want in them. Every bit of desire. Every bit of the emotion I'm too scared to acknowledge.

As his breathing hastens he pulls abruptly out of my mouth and takes hold of himself.

"On the bed," he rasps out and I quickly stand and move to lie down on the soft comforter. Ben follows, and as he kneels between my legs, he jerks that beautiful cock hard and fast until, with a loud grunt he explodes, painting my pussy in his cum. My mouth waters at the sight. He reaches down and roughly takes hold of my neck, pulling me up he crushes his mouth to mine, his tongue sliding along my own. Pulling away he closes his eyes before meeting my gaze.

"I love you."

"We'll have three blowjobs please, mister intoxicologist!" Cassidy raises her voice to be heard above the noise in the crowded bar, as I almost choke on my own spit at her order. If only she knew.

After slamming down our shots, we head out to the dance floor and get lost in the music. I close my eyes and forget about everyone and everything as I move my body to the sensual rhythm.

All too soon I feel myself being dragged back to reality as Wyatt pulls on my arm and leans in to tell me they're heading back to the bar for more drinks. Deciding I could definitely do with some more alcohol, I take hold of her hand and follow her and Cassidy. Grabbing our drinks, we manage to secure ourselves a table and while Cassidy and Wyatt stand, I sit down. My feet immediately begin to ache and I curse myself for my rookie mistake. Every woman knows that once you sit down the pain of heels multiplies by a million, and standing in them again is near impossible.

Sighing, I take a big sip of my Pina Colada and try to listen as Cass and Wyatt catch up on all the gossip. But it's useless. "IloveyouIloveyouIloveyouIloveyou," the words are on a constant rotation in my brain. He loves me. And I love him. Did I tell him that? No. Because I am so freaking scared about what is happening between us.

"Ben told me he loves me," I say the words so quietly that I don't think there is a chance of either of them hearing me. But both women stop talking immediately and swing their heads toward me.

"Hells to the fucking yeah!" Cassidy screeches as Wyatt jumps up and down and wraps me up in a giant, all-consuming hug. It takes them a moment to realize I'm not sharing their excitement, and in fact tears have begun to silently slide down my cheeks.

Wyatt pulls me in for another hug, this one even tighter than the last, and whispers in my ear, "It's okay, Skye. You're okay, sweetie."

Was I though? My inability to trust in Ben's love made me feel broken. He has never given me one reason to doubt him, so why do I find it so hard to believe he could love me?

Cassidy comes over and sits down next to me, taking hold of my hand and looking me straight in the eye.

"You need to cut this shit out, Balls. I love you, but you are not going to wake up one day and magically be over all of these bullshit hang ups you've been holding on to since your dad left. I don't know if that's what you're waiting for, but it's never going to happen like that. The only way to move forward, is to just move forward. Be scared. Be fucking terrified. But be brave enough to still go for it. Ben deserves that. Fuck, you deserve that."

Wyatt leans into me and places her head on my shoulder.

"Skye, please don't let your fear rule you. You could miss out on a lifetime of happiness because you're scared of one moment of pain. If it's real, if it's honest and true, you will work through those moments. They'll be tiny insignificant blips. But the happiness? Sweetie, the happiness will bring you to your knees, and will make every blip worth it." Wyatt's voice wavers slightly and I can feel a quiet pain emanating from her.

Looking between my two best friends, I remember Ben's face as he said those words to me. He is in this, he is in one hundred percent, and he has been from the beginning. It's time I man up and go all in too.

Draining the last of my cocktail, I hold my empty glass up and say, "Right, one more and then I'm going home. I have something I need to do."

Buzzing up to Ben's apartment, my heart hammers in my chest. I sent him a text earlier so I know he's home. Hearing his voice on the intercom telling me to come up, my heart rate kicks up even further, if that's possible. The elevator ride to his seventh-floor apartment is the longest three minutes of my life, but then suddenly I am standing in front of his door and ringing the bell. He pulls the door open wearing only a pair of black boxer briefs, but before I can get distracted by the vision in front of me, I throw my arms around his neck and place a luscious kiss on his mouth. Pulling back, I look him directly in the eye so he can feel the absolute certainty of what I'm about to say.

"I love you, Ben."

A slow, lazy smile spreads across his face.

"I know, Squeak. I was just waiting for you to figure it out."

CHAPTER ELEVEN

*B*en: Baby, you there?

    Skye: Yep.

Ben: Meet me at the entrance to the Botanical Gardens in an hour okay?

Skye: Are we having a picnic?

Ben: Squeak, just meet me there okay, no questions.

Skye: Ugh.

Skye: *Fine*

He's late. Okay only five minutes, but still. Yesterday was our six-month anniversary and Ben had warned me to be ready for a surprise today. One problem though, I hate surprises and had been trying to weasel information out of him since the moment he told me, much to his chagrin.

Suddenly, I am lifted off my feet from behind, held up by strong arms and my favorite face in the whole world is nuzzling into my neck, peppering it with kisses.

"Sorry I'm late, baby, traffic was shit. You ready?"

"Am I ready? Ready for what?" Turning around and taking hold of Ben's face with both my hands, I pull him down to my level. "Tell me! I need to know!"

This elicits a loud laugh from him and grabbing my hand in his, his only response is, "Patience, Squeak, patience."

Guiding me to the street, I enjoy the sensation of my hand in his. One thing I've learned about Ben is that he is fond of the PDA's and is constantly touching me. I'm not going to lie, I love it. Growing up, neither of my parents were particularly affectionate, so I wasn't the most tactile person. But every time Ben touches me, it ignites something and I crave more.

Reaching the street, I find he has a cab waiting and we clamber into it, our hands never disconnecting. The taxi takes off without waiting for directions and I figure Ben has already filled him in on our destination. There goes my chance at a clue.

Ben begins chatting away, and I try to follow but my attention is firmly on the streets outside, hoping to scope out where we are headed.

"Skye!" My attention quickly focuses back on the man sitting next to me when I hear the exasperation in his voice.

"What?" I respond innocently.

"This is really bothering you, isn't it? Not knowing where we're going?"

"I'm sorry!" I hide my face in his shoulder in embarrassment. "I know you're trying to do something really sweet but the not knowing is killing me." Removing my face from the warmth of his body, I look him sadly in the eye. "I'm a terrible girlfriend, aren't I?"

Snorting, he replies, "You're not a terrible girlfriend. Just a control freak. Luckily you have many redeeming qualities that make up for it." He plants a soft kiss on my lips that makes me all tingly. When he takes my bottom lip between his teeth and gently bites down, tugging and then licking away the sting, the tingles intensify and I pull away before I lose control and start to dry hump him right here in this cab.

"Okay, since the surprise aspect isn't working for you, I guess I'll have to let you know what I have planned. Happy?"

"Yes, very. Thank you," I reply with sincerity and turn my body excitedly, almost bouncing in my seat, ready to hear his plans for the day.

"Well, I wanted to plan a day that would be special to you, and I figured since you're so book obsessed we could do a literary tour of New York and check out some of the city's best landmarks. What do you think?"

The note of uncertainty in his voice squeezes at my heart and this moment right here is my undoing. Any lingering doubts about my feelings dissipate at the sound of that tiny waver in his voice, and I know without a shadow of a doubt that I am going to love this man for the rest of my life, no matter what happens between us.

"I think I love you," is my easy reply.

The day that follows is an incredible whirlwind of activity and laughter. We start the day by heading to the Bronx and exploring Edgar Allen Poe's cottage, which I can't believe I have never visited before. The sight of the tiny cottage leaves me speechless and I have goosebumps as we tour it with our wonderful guide, Glen. There are only a couple of other people wandering around the cottage while we are there which adds to the atmosphere, and I feel like I could spend the entire day here, devouring all the knowledge that Glen has to impart. I am in absolute awe of everything I see and learn, but whenever I look Ben's way his eyes are glued firmly on me, following my every movement and appreciating my enthusiasm the same way I am appreciating this experience.

All too soon, the tour is over and after exploring the cottage on our own multiple times, Ben pulls me outside and we head for the subway.

The rest of the day is spent exploring Left Bank Books, where I spend hours trawling through rare books and first editions with the kind of reverence one would expect from a devout bibliophile, followed by the New York Public Library where we examine the current collections on display, and engage in some healthy debates.

Basically, I spend the day trying to control my book whore boner.

Leaving the library, Ben leads me down the steps

and guides me to the street where we take the Line 28 bus to our final destination, Central Park.

We spend the last hours of daylight in the park, taking in the Shakespeare garden before heading for the literary walk, which we stroll along leisurely, enjoying the beauty of the canopy the elms create.

"Today has been amazing, Ben, thank you so much." Holding onto his hand, I pull his arm to me and lean into him, brushing a kiss across his shoulder.

"One more surprise, Squeak," he replies softly and gives me a smile that melts both my heart and my panties.

I'm about to reply when my attention is drawn to the giant carousel in front of us and my heart swells in love and gratitude.

"You remembered," I whisper as I recall the conversation we had months ago when I shared with him my happiest memory. The moment that happened right here on the carousel in front of us, with my mom and dad. They had been so happy that day, carefree and so unlike their usual selves. The vision I had of them sitting in one of the carriages with me in between them, while they laughed and joked was something I will never forget, and a memory I clung to every time the sadness had overwhelmed me.

"I remember everything you say, Squeak." Leaning his forehead against mine, he kisses my nose. With a big smile lighting up his face he grabs my hand and drags me toward the ride. "You ready to ride, cowgirl?" he throws over his shoulder and I groan at his attempt at humor.

"Ugh, will your jokes ever get better?"

"Probably not." His laughter hits my ears as a smile blooms across my face.

Later, as we sit on the subway headed home, I relax against Ben. Exhausted but sated, I am so grateful to the man beside me. I've never had someone want to take care of me the way he does. The feeling of adoration is all encompassing and I wonder now how I ever lived without him in my life. This thought momentarily jolts me out of my blissed stupor as my mind wanders into dangerous territory. How will I survive if this ends and I'm left abandoned again?

Looking up at Ben, I watch as he scrolls through his phone replying to emails, and I shut down that train of thought immediately. This is real, I tell myself. This is forever, and I'm not going to create trouble where there is none.

Glancing up, Ben smiles at me.

"You good?" he asks.

"Yep," I reply. "Ben?"

"Yeah, baby?"

"You are so getting laid tonight." I silence his laughter with my mouth.

CHAPTER TWELVE

I feel the sun shining down on me as I walk along 14th Street, humming the tune to Helium under my breath and trying to control the excitement thrumming through my veins.

Ben has proven over the last six months that he is the king of surprises. Whether it's popping into my work unannounced, randomly sending me flowers or planning something special like our day on the weekend. He is forever doing things that make me feel cherished and loved.

So, today I am determined to earn some brownie points, and as I make my way through the doors to UTCB Software Solutions, I am carrying a box of Guinness, Whiskey and Irish Cream cupcakes from Ben's favorite bakery. I'm hoping to drag him from work early so we can enjoy a night of pizza and Netflix. Hopefully followed by me for dessert.

The elevator doors open and I step out, following the path I took on my previous, and only, visit to Ben's office, I am taken through an open-plan floor space filled with about a dozen cubicles. The low hum of noise that is unique to an office workplace is somewhat soothing and I can easily see Ben, confident and comfortable in this environment. The thought makes my chest puff with a sense of pride that I have a small claim on this man.

Approaching his office door, I am juggling the box of cupcakes to free up a hand so I can knock when I hear the sound of voices and I pause to ensure I'm not interrupting anything important.

"Ben, you're a genius! I've been trying to debug that source code for days and was completely stuck."

At the sound of the feminine voice I peek through the door and see a beautiful blonde sitting on the edge of Ben's desk. Tall and lean, her crossed legs appear to go on forever and my eyes trail up them, taking in her elegant black dress. Sitting at knee length with a small slit along the side and a V neck that dips low enough to show off a slight amount of cleavage, the overall effect is professional yet sexy.

My eyes rise to her face and I see a classically beautiful woman; her face made up impeccably and her long blonde hair pulled up into an intricate chignon. She is basically the polar opposite to my short, curvy self with my boho style and lack of makeup, and I feel the icy tentacles of jealousy start to tighten around my heart. I can't compete with a woman like this and as I watch the two of them, I observe her mannerisms closely. The way she brushes her hand across her chest, drawing attention to her breasts. The small, seemingly innocuous touches she places on Ben. Her entire demeanour towards him makes it clear that her interest is not purely professional.

As I stand in the doorway silently observing, Ben glances up and notices me.

"Skye! Baby, what are you doing here?" He is out of his chair, bounding across the room and wrapping me up in a hug before I have a chance to respond. His enthusiastic welcome almost causes me to drop the cupcakes, but I'm too relieved at his open display of affection in front of Glamor Girl to care, and glancing past Ben I see her watching us with barely concealed disdain.

"What did you bring me, babe?" Ben asks, reaching out and taking the box from my hands, he holds it in one large palm while he laces the fingers of his other hand through mine and pulls me into his office.

Placing the cupcakes on his desk, he holds me tight to his side and addresses GG.

"Squeak, this is Siobhan; she's the assistant project manager on that account I've been heading. Siobhan, this is my girl, Skye." He looks down at me, planting a kiss on the top of my head. Trying to be adult about the situation, I give Siobhan a warm smile and hold my hand out to her.

"It's so nice to meet you."

"Yes, you too," she replies in a silky voice that doesn't quite match the glint of malice in her eyes.

"Okay, Ben, I'll leave you to it now. The hotel bookings are all confirmed and our flight is ten fifteen on Wednesday morning. I'll have a car pick myself up and then we'll be at your place at about seven thirty. Have a lovely evening." She reaches out, stroking down Ben's arm and giving it a squeeze before nodding to me with a slight smirk tilting her lips and walking out.

I shoot Ben a quizzical look before questioning, "Hotel?"

"Yeah, the managing directors of the company we're doing that project for sent a memo today, requesting a face-to-face meeting to go over the finer points of the analysis we've given them." He pulls a face, letting me know he's as thrilled about it as I am. Although remembering the predatory look in Siobhan's eyes as she watched Ben, I'm guessing my apathy beats his.

"So, where are you heading?" I probe for details, doing my best to appear unconcerned.

"Their head office is in Atlanta, so all going to plan I'll be back Thursday. You think you can live without me and my bad jokes for one night, babe?"

Trying to hide the turmoil consuming me, I tilt my head as if pondering his question. "I think I just might be able to survive one night." I allow a little snort to escape.

"That's my girl." He crushes me to him in a toe-tingling, full-body hug. "Now, what's in your box?" He waggles his eyebrows at me and I can't control the loud groan that bursts from my mouth.

"Yeah, I don't think a night off from those jokes is going to be a struggle at all."

"Ah, Squeak, you know it's all part of my charm." Handing me the box, he picks up his jacket with one hand and wraps the other arm around my shoulders.

"C'mon, babe, I've earned an early finish. Let's get out of here."

Lying on the sofa, the entire length of my body is connected to Ben's as we laze about in a food coma, watching a Big Bang Theory marathon. But my mind is elsewhere and I've struggled to stay present all night. I keep seeing Siobhan's hand gripping Ben's arm, hearing her melodic voice play over and over in my head as I analyze everything I heard her say. I hate myself for letting these insecurities plague me but I'm helpless to stop them.

"Skye?" Ben's whisper caresses my ear.

"Huh?" I answer distractedly.

"Baby, is everything okay? You've been preoccupied all night."

I squeeze my eyes shut for a moment, trying to center myself and find the courage to have this conversation. Because we do need to have it, of that I'm completely sure.

Manoeuvring myself and twisting my body so that I am facing him, I reach up and stroke my hand gently across his cheek. He leans into my touch, never breaking eye contact, waiting patiently for me to continue.

"Did I ever tell you my dad met his new wife at work?"

"No," he whispers. "You never mentioned that."

"Yeah, Genevieve was his secretary. It's so ridiculously cliché, it's hard not to laugh." I close my eyes against the inevitable pain that flows whenever I think about my father. I feel Ben brush his nose along mine and then ghost a kiss across my cheek. It's only then that I realize a tear has escaped.

"Siobhan has feelings for you," I say, my voice barely audible.

"Yes, she does," he confirms, and my eyes snap to his in shock.

"You know?"

"Well, yeah. I'm an incredibly perceptive guy, you know." I bow my head down, placing it against his chest, allowing his warmth to comfort me. Placing a finger under my chin, he lifts my head up so I can meet his gaze. "Plus, she told me at last year's Christmas party." He gives me a lopsided grin that causes me to reach up and kiss him. Licking along the seam of his lips, I seek entry. He opens his mouth and his tongue finds mine. We continue like this, Ben's possession of my mouth slowly driving away any doubts I have about our relationship, reaffirming his want, his desire. His need for me.

Breaking away, he nibbles and kisses along my jaw and neck before resting his forehead against mine and closing his eyes.

"I'm not your dad, Skye. I don't want Siobhan, I want you. Every bit of you, including your trust. I need you to know that I will never intentionally do anything to hurt you. I love you, Squeak. You need to trust that or you'll create problems that don't exist."

"I know," I murmur. "I'll try, I promise."

"Good. But just in case you need more reassurance, let's see what I can do" He presses his body into mine and every synapse jolts to life.

Placing a soft kiss on my temple, he says, "I love the way your mind works, the way you look at things so differently from me, and see things I don't."

His hand slides up my body, pausing briefly to squeeze my breast and pinch my nipple, it ends its delicious path resting on my chest.

"I love your heart. The way you love so hard and so fast. Your passion for the ones lucky enough to be loved by you." He leans down, planting a kiss beside where his hand lays.

Glancing up at me, I see the playful look in his eyes vanish, replaced by a look of pure lust. His mouth takes mine in a crushing display of ownership and I welcome it. I want to be owned by him. To be his.

"This ass. These tits. This mouth. Your body is fucking incredible and I love that you trust me with it. It makes me want to dirty it up in every possible way, before loving it back to pure. Can I dirty you up, baby? I need to so bad." His voice is low and harsh, pulsing with want.

"Please," I sigh. That is all the encouragement he needs and his hands are immediately tugging my sleep shorts, along with my panties, down my legs and throwing them across the room. I shiver as the cold air hits my lower body, my pussy throbbing, and Ben slides a finger through my slit as a low growling sound vibrates from his throat.

"So fucking wet for me." His hand makes its way up

my body and finds itself at my neck and lightly squeezes. "Only for me, Squeak, yeah?"

"Yes," I answer without hesitation. Because there is none. No man has ever turned me on the way Ben does.

Pulling his cock out of his boxers he pumps it slowly before using the tip to tease through my arousal, and I moan as my body is taken hostage by the overwhelming sensations. Reaching down, I push his hand away and take hold of my favorite appendage. My hand looks tiny and my fingers don't even meet but I hold firm, jerking him off and loving the curses that trip off his lips.

Reaching over me, he grabs his wallet off the coffee table, quickly removing his emergency condom. Sheathing himself expertly, he pulls my leg up and over his hip and thrusts his cock deep inside me with no preamble. The close proximity of our bodies causes his pubic bone to rub against my clit with every thrust and the feeling sends me reeling. I'm desperate. Chasing my release, I claw at his back in a futile attempt to anchor myself.

"Feels so good, Skye, your cunt's so fucking tight, squeezing me like this. You like having my dick pound into you?"

"Ah, harder, Ben. I need more." He grasps my ass with both hands and slams himself into me, deep and hard, he is hitting every spot that I need. That I crave.

I lose the power to talk as wave after wave of pleasure rides through my body. Ben's head falls forward, landing in the crook of my shoulder. He bites down hard as his cock pulses out his release and my pussy milks every last drop.

I don't know how long we lie like that, wrapped up in each other, enjoying the intimacy, but I can't remember ever feeling this way before.

Then, lifting his head, Ben places his lips lightly against mine. "It's you, Squeak. I just want you."

And just like that, I have found my happy place.

CHAPTER THIRTEEN

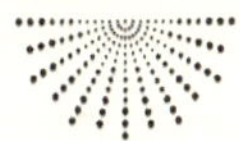

$\mathcal{N}$o. The word bounces around my brain as it refuses to understand what it's seeing on my phone screen.

"So, he's behind me, pounding into me like he thinks he's a fucking porn star, when he pulls out and rips off the condom. And that's hot, right? I love it when a guy comes on me. So, I turn around to watch and he shoots cum right into my ear. My ear, Balls! Into my fucking ear! It took seven fucking q-tips to get that shit out!"

No, no, no, no, no, no, no.

"Skye! Are you even listening to me?"

"What?" I reply, though my eyes remain glued to the screen in front of me, as if staring at it long enough will change the notification glaring at me.

"Seriously, Skyballs? Sext with Spanky on your own time, you're supposed to be mine tonight."

Finally raising my eyes to meet Cassidy's across the table, she cocks her head in realisation that I am upset.

"Babes, what's wrong?" Reaching out, her hand grabs mine and gives it a reassuring squeeze.

"I'm late."

"What? Late for what?" The confused look on her face would be laughable if my world wasn't crashing down around me right now.

Shoving my phone in her face with the period tracker notification front and center, I feel the sting of tears as I scramble to make sense of this.

"You're late," she repeats quietly.

"Yep."

"But it's only a week, Balls, that's nothing. It's probably nothing."

"I'm never late, Cass. Like never never. I can't... I mean, I just... What do I do?" I ask, and my voice sounds tiny, even to my own ears.

Squaring her shoulders, she sucks in a deep breath before replying. "We get up, we find the nearest pharmacy, we buy a pregnancy test and you pee all over that fucker. Then we worry about what to do next. Sound like a plan?"

"Sounds like a plan," I reply softly, standing up and taking hold of Cassidy's proffered hand. "Cass? Thank you."

"Enough with the sap, Balls, my cold heart can't handle it. Now let's get out of here."

❦

"Get out."

"What, no way! Jesus, Skyballs, don't be shy, just

hike the skirt up, yank the panties down and pee on the goddam stick. I want to find out if I'm going to be a motherfucking aunt!"

"I am not peeing in front of you. That is not happening, so if you want to find out, you need to leave."

"Ugh, hurry up then." Huffing out a noise of frustration, she turns on her heel and storms out, slamming the door behind her.

Turning the box in my hands, I read the instructions on the pregnancy test for the twenty-seventh time before situating myself on the toilet and waiting for the two bottles of water I drank to do their job.

Five minutes later, I'm placing the test on the sink and washing my hands while I call out to Cassidy that it's safe to enter.

"Oh my god, you take forever to pee!" she says as she bursts through the door and crouches down to look at the test. "How long do we have to wait?"

"Three minutes." I slump to the ground as Cassidy checks the clock on her phone.

Coming over to where I sit, she slides down and takes up a spot on the floor next to me. Kissing me on my forehead, she lies her head on my shoulder and links her arm through mine.

"Are you excited?"

I sigh as I consider her question. "I don't know. I mean, Ben and I have never even talked about kids. Or the future at all really. We've only been together for six months, we've just been enjoying each other. And he has that history with his ex tricking him. I honestly don't know how he would take the news of a pregnancy."

"Okay, I'm going to ask you again, and this time I don't want you to think. I just want you to feel. Are you excited?" Cassidy presses.

Unbidden, an image of Ben holding a soft, sleepy baby in his arms appears in my mind's eye and my heart constricts at the thought. "Yeah," I say softly. "I think I am." I allow a small smile to break free.

"Eeeekkk, I'm gonna be an aunty! Aunty Cass! I swear, this kid is so fucking lucky, I'm going to give her chocolate every time I see her. She's going to love me!"

"Her, huh?" I ask, laughing.

"It's totes gonna be a girl, Balls. I know it," she replies confidently.

Looking at my best friend, I feel the dread take flight. Cassidy's excitement is contagious and I start to feel it hum through my body.

"Okay, you ready? Three minutes is up."

"Yep, let's do this."

Cass bounds up and over to the sink, snatching up the test and examining it closely. Her eyes widen as they meet mine.

"We're having a baby! Oh my god, we're having a baby, Balls!" She begins jumping up and down and screaming.

My vision is impaired momentarily by white spots clouding my eyes and for a minute, all I can hear is the sound of my own heartbeat thundering in my ears.

"Oh, ew!" Cassidy shouts, suddenly dropping the test on the floor. "You peed on that!" Those four words bring me back to my senses and a loud laugh escapes as I join her in her happy dance. Because, baby.

A baby.

I'm having a baby.

We're having a baby.

Bring. It. On.

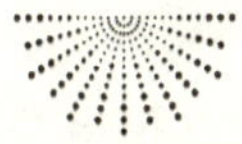

CHAPTER FOURTEEN

My eyes pop open as my phone alarm begins to quietly play on my bedside table, rousing me from my light sleep, and I reach over to silence it before it can wake Ben.

Rolling over to face him, I smile at the peaceful look on his slumbering face and take this moment to consider what I have to do this morning. I should be nervous, but I'm not.

Ben arrived home from his business trip yesterday afternoon and after an intimate dinner at Petite Assiette d'Amour, the restaurant from our first date, we came back to my place and made up for the night we missed. Later, as I lay in bed sated and content, listening to the calming sound of Ben's breathing, my excitement over this morning's announcement grew.

I know this man, I know his heart and I trust fully in our relationship. It's taken me a long time to reach this point, but there is no doubt in my mind that I want this future with Ben.

Unable to contain my excitement any longer, I bounce out of bed and race to the kitchen to put my plan into action.

Reaching up to the overhead cupboard, I pull out the mug I purchased yesterday. I hold it in my right palm as I look it over for the hundredth time, my eyes immediately pulled to the message on the bottom of the cup. You are going to be a DAD! is printed in bold, black lettering, contrasting starkly with the bright white mug and I can't wait to see Ben's face as realization dawns.

Quickly making his morning cup of coffee I make my way back into the bedroom and place the drink on my bedside table. Then jumping on the bed, I bounce over to Ben and begin peppering his face with kisses.

Groaning sleepily, his mouth quirks with a small smile at my attack before he reaches out and grabs me around the waist, pulling me to him and nuzzling my neck.

"Well, that was a fantastic way to wake up," he says, his voice muffled.

Pulling away, I move from the warmth of his body to grab the coffee. "Here you go, I made this for you," I say, thrusting the drink at him with a big grin.

"Uh, okay, thanks, baby," he replies, throwing me a stupefied look and taking a small sip.

The next five minutes are the longest of my life as Ben drinks his coffee slowly, keeping up a steady stream of conversation. About what, I have no idea because all I can hear is the excited thump of my heartbeat in my ears.

"Okay, Squeak, what the hell is going on? You're about to burst out of your skin over there."

"Nothing!" I deny vehemently. "I'm just in a good mood!"

"Right." That single word is dripping with disbelief. "Whatever you say, babe." He finally drains the last of his coffee. My eyes widen in anticipation, and then widen even further as I watch Ben place the mug on his bedside table and move to get up without even glancing inside.

"Wait!" I screech.

Stopping mid turn, he slowly returns his gaze to me, and even in my state of anxiety, I note the teasing expression on his face. "What's up, Squeak?"

"Here." I shove the now-empty mug into his hands. "I don't think you got all the coffee. You should check and make sure there's none left in the bottom."

"Okay," he says, drawing the word out so it contains multiple syllables. He throws me a look that screams 'I'm just humoring you'.

As Ben glances down to the bottom of the mug, I kneel on the bed, right in front of him, practically giddy as I await his reaction.

I see it immediately. The moment his brain registers the words. His eyes shoot to mine and the panic causes an internal flinch.

"What the fuck is this, Skylah?"

Skylah. The use of my full name is like a punch to the stomach. I don't think he's ever used it. Skye, Squeak, Baby, Babe. Those are my names. Not Skylah.

"What do you mean?" I question, my voice losing any trace of excitement.

"What the fuck are you talking about? Is this some kind of fucked up joke?" he questions, brandishing the mug aggressively.

"I'm pregnant," I whisper, and I watch as the color drains from his face right before my eyes.

"What?" The level of his voice matches my own, and if I wasn't so consumed by my own fear of how this scenario is about to play out, my heart would be breaking for him.

Suddenly his eyes shutter and it's as though I'm staring at a stranger. "I'm not marrying you."

The words explode from his mouth brutally. Cruelly. And the force of them pushes me back off my knees leaving me on my ass.

"Wha- I... I don't expect you to." I barely recognize my own voice as it strains to break free. I reach for him instinctively, seeking the comfort that his touch usually provides me, but I watch in horror as he pulls away and glares at me.

"I won't do this again. I won't be forced into something I never asked for. We were safe. Every. Fucking. Time. This shouldn't have happened."

And suddenly my temper is ignited and I raise myself up and square my shoulders. "What exactly are you accusing me of, Ben? Because it sounds an awful lot like you're saying I did this on purpose."

"If the shoe fits," he replies with a shrug of his shoulders.

"How exactly would I do that? Like you said, we

were always safe. The condom always came from you. How exactly would I get pregnant on purpose?" My heart sinks as a thought occurs to me. "Unless you think I'm lying to you right now?"

His hands fly to his hair and he pulls on it, a crazed look of desperation on his face, but he doesn't answer me. He leaves the question lingering in the air.

"Get out." I don't even think, I just talk. "Get out of my home right now." For a fleeting moment I see my Ben. Mine. And the anguish radiating from his eyes just about slays me. However, it's gone before I can even grasp its meaning. My eyes never leave his form as he throws on his clothes and stalks out of the room.

Standing, I move slowly to the bedroom door and observe him as he makes his escape. My heart shatters as I watch him walk away. But he never looks back.

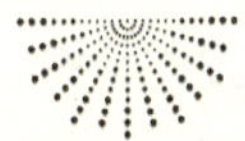

CHAPTER FIFTEEN

My phone buzzes from somewhere on the floor for the millionth time, and I cover my ears to block out the sound. I could get up and silence it, but that would require I move and honestly, that seems impossible right now.

The incessant buzzing continues and I curse Cassidy's persistence. The first few messages raised my hopes. Every time I heard the small chirp from my phone, my heart pounded in anticipation, hopeful that Ben had come to his senses and was reaching out. Instead, disappointment crushed me each time I realized it was Cassidy, looking for a rundown of how this morning had gone. The sound of the phone crashing against the far wall when I throw it gives me a certain sense of satisfaction. For a second. Only for a second.

I close my eyes tightly against the images that are playing on a loop in my mind. Ben's eyes, and the anger that burned in them, are haunting me. Curling myself up into an even tighter ball, I can't control the sobs that are wracking my body.

The front door slams shut, startling me into silence as my breath catches in my throat.

"I'm coming in so you two better not be naked in there!" Cassidy screeches at the top of her lungs and I hear loud, stomping footsteps making their way toward my bedroom. "Yep, heading to the bedroom. I'm almost there. I sure hope there's nobody fucking in there."

My breath escapes in a gust of sadness and the silent tears continue as I hear the door squeak quietly as it opens.

"Shit." The word is whispered so quietly I barely hear it, but suddenly the bed dips and I am wrapped tightly in Cassidy's arms.

We lie like this for what feels like an eternity. I allow her to stroke my hair and soothe me, soaking up everything she is offering me until finally, I feel a tiny bit of my spirit return to my body.

"Cass." I raise my red-rimmed, bloodshot eyes to meet her pained ones. "He hates me."

"Babes, I'm sorry," she sighs. "If it helps, I'm going to kill him. I'm seriously going to kill him hard. Like, google the most torturous methods and all kinds of shit."

I permit myself a small smile at that and if I wasn't so angry I'd probably feel bad for him. Cassidy is not to be messed with.

"What do you need? Tell me what I can do."

"I don't know," I answer honestly, swiping at the tears that continue to escape.

"He accused me of trying to trap him, Cass, of trying to get him to marry me by getting pregnant." As I admit this, I realize that's the most painful thing of all. That someone I thought knew me, someone I thought cared about me, could accuse me of something I would never do. It's like a punch to the heart every time I think about it. "How could he think I would do that?"

"I'm sure he was just shocked, Skyballs, you know he would never think that if he was in his right frame of mind." She pulls me in tighter, surrounding me with her warmth. "But that's no excuse, and I'm still going to make a little coin purse out of his balls," she says into the top of my head.

I pause for a beat before whispering, "I fucking love you, Cass."

"Language, Balls! Nobody likes a motherfucking potty mouth," she scoffs. Feeling a small laugh bubbling up, I allow myself a brief moment of respite from the heaviness that has consumed me since the moment Ben's eyes locked onto the bottom of that ridiculous mug.

"Okay, babes, time to woman up. Your doctor appointment is at one forty-five, right? You need to have a shower and wash the stank off and then I'll come with you."

Instinctively, my head starts to shake from side to side and I'm about to argue with her when she cuts me off before I can start.

"Don't even try it, Skylah. We're going. Now, are

you going to get up by yourself, or do I need to help you?" Remembering the giant bruise I was left with the last time she "helped" me out of bed, I quickly scramble to my feet and head for the bathroom.

�

"I'm sorry, what?" my grip on Cassidy's hand tightens as I try to make sense of what the doctor is telling me.

"You're not pregnant, Skye, I'm very sorry." The sincerity shines bright in Dr. McLean's eyes.

The blood rushes to my head, pounding through my ears. It's now all I can hear and I struggle to catch my breath as the doctor's words hang in the air.

"Skye, babes are you okay? Skye, look at me." Cassidy's anxious voice reaches my ears but it sounds muffled, as if it's floating from a long distance. My manic eyes meet hers as I lose the last bit of control over my body and I start trying to gasp in huge gulps of air. My throat is constricting and I begin to panic as I can't seem to get enough oxygen.

"Skye!"

Not pregnant, not pregnant. I'm not pregnant.

My glazed eyes note Cassidy kneeling in front of me. I see her hands grasping my face trying to pull my focus to her, but I can't feel them.

"Skye! Look at me, look at me, babes."

I lost him for no reason. There's no baby. I don't even get to keep a tiny part of him. Not pregnant. No baby.

"Breathe, Skye, take slow deep breaths. Deep

breaths, Skye." I hear the doctor's calm voice calling out to me.

My chest is heaving, and I'm fighting for breath when Cassidy roughly pulls my face towards her and leans her forehead against mine.

"Balls, focus on my voice. You're okay, just take deep breaths and calm down." Her voice is firm and composed, and I focus purely on that as she repeats the same words by rote.

Slowly my body becomes my own again, my breathing slows and air fills my lungs. The buzzing in my ears stops as my vision clears.

I see Cassidy, still kneeling in the same position in front of me and notice the doctor hunched over to my right, rubbing her hand over my back reassuringly. Once I have regained control, both Cassidy and the doctor return to their seats and Cass immediately reaches over, taking hold of my hand and squeezing.

"If I'm not pregnant, why did the test come out positive?" Even I can hear the note of desperation in my voice.

"Home pregnancy tests are generally highly reliable these days, however they're not infallible, and false positives do sometimes occur. Most likely it was a chemical issue."

I nod as though I understand. As if my heart isn't breaking. "I'm going to give you ladies a moment. Please take your time." She stalks out of the office.

We sit there in silence, letting the last half hour sink in fully.

"I wanted that baby."

My whisper sounds loud in the quiet room and I feel warm tears trailing down my cheeks.

"I know you did, Balls."

"I lost him for no reason." My eyes widen in horror as realization dawns. "He's going to think he was right, Cassidy! He's going to think I lied about being pregnant!"

Cassidy takes in my panicked expression calmly. "I don't think he will, Skye. I really think when he calms down, he's going to realize how big he fucked up, and come crawling back. Then you'll make him suffer a bit for being the huge thundercunt he was, before forgiving him and living happily ever after."

"And if he doesn't?" I ask.

"If he doesn't? Then fuck the douchedick. Fuck him hard, rough and without lube." And with that she rises, pulling me out of my seat and linking her arm with mine as we exit the doctor's office, without looking back.

CHAPTER SIXTEEN

I reach down and pull another book from my pile, the repetitive actions of stocking the shelves is calming me, but my movements are slow and stilted.

It's been four days since my world imploded, and I'm still trying to make sense of what happened. I had hoped that returning to work today would provide a distraction, but I can't seem to focus on anything but my own grief.

I know that I need to get in touch with Ben and tell him there's no baby. I know the longer I leave it, the worse it's going to look, but I can't bring myself to make the call just yet. The accusatory look in his eyes still torments me and I'm not ready to face it again. Not now, when I am mourning what feels like a very real loss.

A gentle tap on my shoulder startles me and the book I am holding slips from my grasp. Turning, I am shocked to see Mason behind me.

"Hi, Skye," he says, giving me a small smile. "I'm sorry to ambush you like this, but I was wondering if you would have lunch with me? If you have the time?"

I'm taken aback by his request. Hell, I'm taken aback by his very presence. One thing I've learned over the last six months is that Mason Alexander is a workaholic, and it's rare to find him outside of the office. Which can only mean that this is important, and my heart picks up speed as I consider his request. My instinct is to say no. That I'm not ready to hear anything he has to say, but he is studying me with a quiet intensity and I can almost feel him willing me to accept.

"Okay," I say with a sigh. "Let me just tell Tanya that I'm heading out." He nods in agreement and moves to wait by the front door.

After a brief moment with my assistant manager, I join Mason, and without a word we make our way to the street outside where we are immediately swallowed up by the crowd.

I let the noises of New York distract me; anything to avoid thinking about the conversation that is looming, as we instinctively follow the path forged by the strangers ahead of us.

Mason stops suddenly and draws my attention to a small cafe tucked away in a quiet alley. I nod my approval, and we make our way inside. The eatery is quiet and I'm grateful for it, this is not a conversation I want to have in a loud, chaotic environment so I send a silent thank you to Mason for his considerate choice.

We take a seat and our orders are promptly taken

by a perky brunette, who I find myself silently loathing, for no other reason than her happiness makes my misery seem so much more tangible.

"So, are you his little messenger boy?" Unable to tolerate the silence any more, my voice is tinged with bitterness.

Mason looks down at his hands. A small smile plays on his lips, but it doesn't quite reach his eyes. They hold only sadness.

"No. He doesn't know I'm here, I promise."

"What are you doing here, Mason?" I question.

"He's not doing so well," he replies quietly, and the tone of his voice causes me to flinch, but I try to hold tight to my anger.

"I didn't do this to him, Mason, he created this shit storm," I hiss. "Do you have any idea how excited I was to tell him about the baby? How excited I was about the future I thought we were going to have?" I stop abruptly as I feel my throat tighten and tears threaten.

"He was an asshole, Skye. I'm not denying that. Fuck, I'm sure that even he knows it. But I'm asking you to cut him some slack. You know what he went through with Amber, can you give him some time? Let him get his head back together? But please don't write him off."

The waitress appears next to the table with our food, and an uneasy silence descends as she places my chicken salad and Mason's roast beef sandwich in front of us.

Once we are alone again, I allow Mason's words to

settle, and I can't help but be reminded of Ben's words to me, "I'm not your dad, Skye."

"I'm not Amber, Mason. I don't deserve to be punished for her mistakes." I close my eyes as Ben's face comes to mind, and I remember the anger that tainted it during our confrontation. "How could he say that? How could he believe I would do that to him?" I whisper.

Reaching across the table, Mason gives my hand a quick squeeze. "He doesn't, Skye, but he's too fucking wrapped up in his own pain to see yours. Listen, when all that shit with Amber went down, it messed him up pretty bad. He had made peace with the future he thought was being forced on him. He had somehow managed to not only be okay with it, but he was excited. He wanted that baby, and he had even convinced himself that he had a future with her." Mason spits out the word her as if it leaves a bitter taste in his mouth. "When the truth came out, he was crushed. I've never seen him like that before." He raises his eyes to meet mine. "Until now."

Sliding my gaze away, I mull over his words. I know Ben loves me. Somehow throughout all of this I have held tight to that fact. I know he's lashing out, but knowing it and accepting it are two very different things.

"He should have talked to me, not just run away." My voice has regained its strength, and I talk with conviction. "He asked me to trust him, Mason, to trust his love for me. I deserve that same trust." I push my chair back and get up to leave.

Pausing, I take in Mason's disheartened face and try to maintain my composure. "When he's ready to talk, I'll listen. I'll always hear him out. But I'm not sure I can ever forgive him for this."

Hurrying out of the cafe, I make it halfway back to Books & Beans before the tears start to fall.

CHAPTER SEVENTEEN

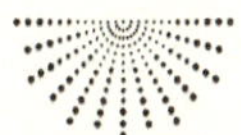

*B*en: Can I see you?
Ben: I need to see you, Skye.
Ben: Please.

I'm standing on the stoop to Ben's building, trying to work up the nerve to ring his buzzer, but my body feels numb and I'm overwhelmed with anxiety. It's been a week since I last saw him, and while I knew this meeting was inevitable, that doesn't make it any easier.

The front door is thrown open by a harried woman who is being dragged forward by two young children. They are practically vibrating with excitement, ready for whatever adventures the day holds for them. I grab hold of the door as my eyes follow the little bundles of energy, racing down the street. My heart aches as my vision clouds, and I see an image of Ben being pulled along by a little girl with light brown curls in my mind's eye.

Shaking my head to clear it, I move forward into the building and steel myself for what is about to happen.

I'm terrified to tell Ben that there is no baby. Terrified to hear that venom in his voice again. But as I leave the elevator and make my way down the hall to Ben's door, I prepare myself for exactly that.

I knock hesitantly, and as I hear his footsteps approach, I make one last silent prayer that I can do what needs to be done.

The door is pulled open and I can only stare in shock at Ben's haggard appearance. His eyes are red and bloodshot as though he hasn't slept in days, and he is sporting a full beard. My hands itch to reach out to him, to caress his cheek as I lean into his body, and try to catch a hint of his familiar scent. However, I contain myself and my hands stay where they are, locked to my side.

"Hey," Ben says, offering me a tight smile. His voice is rough, as though talking is difficult, but I refuse to consider how hard this week may have been for him. Instead, I focus on the intensity of my own heartbreak, and allow the anger to clear my head while Ben stands there drinking me in. "Sorry, come in." He steps back to give me room to enter.

I walk in and pause just inside the entry, unsure how to proceed. Looking around, the sadness practically crushes me. We have created so many memories here over the last six months, and the realization that this is probably the last time I'll stand here, the last time I'll see him, is destroying me.

"Have a seat." Ben points to the overstuffed sofa in the living area. "Can I get you a drink? Coffee? Soda or water?"

"No, I'm fine, thanks," I reply as I take a seat.

Ben crosses the room quickly and sits himself down on the coffee table, right in front of me. Our knees graze, barely touching, but it's enough to cause my breath to catch in my throat.

Trying to refocus, I close my eyes and consider how I'm going to start this conversation. Ben beats me to the punch, though.

"I fucked up, Squeak." My eyes snap open and meet his briefly, before he scrubs his hands across his face and continues. "So bad. I fucked everything up so bad, and I'm sorry. I don't even…" His voice drifts off. "I've been fucking trying to figure out how to fix this for the last four days but I've got nothing." Reaching over he takes hold of my hands and laces our fingers together, his eyes glued to the perfect fit. "You telling me about our baby should have been a fucking spectacular moment, and I ruined it. I can never take that back but I promise you—"

"There is no baby." My voice cracks as I abruptly cut him off, and I watch as his eyes cloud over. As the pain of losing another baby he didn't know he wanted, sets in.

"I don't understand." His eyes search mine for answers, while mine search his for reproach.

"It was a false positive. When we went to the doctor

the test came back negative. She said that it happens sometimes." I can hear the desperation in my voice. The need for him to trust my truth. To believe me. To believe in me.

His hands tighten around mine and suddenly I'm in motion, my body pulled to his and his arms enveloping me.

"I'm so sorry. Are you okay?" he whispers into my hair, his warm breath tickling my ear. I pull back, and meeting his gaze, I try to ascertain his sincerity.

"You believe me?"

"Fuck, Skye, of course I believe you. I know you would never do that, lie about something so huge. I know you, Squeak." He cups my face with his large hands and gently places his forehead against mine.

"I was an asshole, and I lost my head, my fucking mind, for a minute there. But I know you would never pull the shit that Amber did. I'm so sorry I questioned that."

With that he closes the small gap between us and brushes his lips against mine. The kiss starts soft, but as soon as his tongue tastes mine, our control snaps. I put every bit of emotion that has pulsed through my body this past week, into that kiss. And for a brief moment, I let the hungry desperation consume me, and allow the heat of Ben's mouth to convince me that we are going to be okay.

But as I pull away all I can taste is regret, and might-have-beens.

"We can try, if you like." Ben's low voice interrupts my thoughts.

"Try what?"

"For a baby. I know it's not something we had ever talked about, but if it's what you want…"

"Wait, Ben, stop for a second." I force the words out harshly, scarcely believing the change in his attitude. "We can't just act like this never happened. A week ago, you accused me of trying to trap you with a baby. You spoke to me as if you hated me. You looked at me as though I disgusted you! I don't know if I can forgive you for that."

"Yes, you can." His eyes beseech me. "You have to, Squeak. I fucked up, I couldn't possibly have fucked up any bigger. I know that. I let shit from my past fuck me up, but I love you. You know I love you."

"You left me," I whisper. "I trusted you. I believed you when you said you wouldn't hurt me. But you did. You crushed me."

His body moves closer to mine, almost imperceptibly, while I speak. His legs now splayed on either side of mine, his face only inches away. I place a hand on his cheek and feel him lean into my touch. My eyes seek his, and as I gaze at the man before me, I remember the boy he was. The boy who helped me see the sunshine on my darkest day. Who would have thought that all these years later, he would be the one to bring the storm?

"I need time. I'm sorry, but I need to figure out if I can move on from this."

He closes his eyes, but not before I glimpse the pain radiating from them, and my heart cracks with the knowledge that I am hurting him. But I need to do this.

If we are to have any chance of surviving, I need to be sure I can forgive him, and he needs to be sure that he really does trust me.

This time it's me that closes the space between us, and I place a kiss on his full mouth, attempting to soften the blow.

"I won't lose you, Squeak. I'm not going to just give up."

For the first time in a week, a genuine smile lights up my face.

"Well, you wouldn't be the man I fell in love with if you did." I rise and head for the door.

"You said we." His voice stops me in my tracks.

"What?" I question.

"You said when we went to the doctor. Who's we?"

"Oh, Cassidy went with me."

"Oh shit."

"Yeah, I suggest you wear a cup next time you see her. She's kind of gunning for your balls."

A smile plays on his lips, but it doesn't quite reach his eyes.

"It should've been me with you," he says, and the irrefutable sadness in his voice almost undoes me. "I really wish it had been me."

I nod my head in agreement and before he can say anything else I make my exit.

Once outside in the hall, I lean against his closed door, and as the tears escape, I whisper, "I do too."

CHAPTER EIGHTEEN

*S*aturday 10/7

Ben: Knock, knock.
    Ben: Knock, knock.
    Ben: Knock, knock.
    Ben: Knock, knock.
    Ben: Knock, knock.
    Skye: No one's home.

Wednesday 10/11

Ben: Knock, knock.
    Ben: Knock, knock.
    Ben: Knock, knock.

Skye: Ugh, who's there?
Ben: Britney Spears.
Skye: Britney Spears who?
Ben: Knock, knock.
Skye: Who's there?
Ben: Oops I did it again.
Ben: I miss you, Squeak.

&a,

Sunday 10/15

Ben: Knock, knock.
　　Skye: Who's there?
　　Ben: A broken pencil.
　　Skye: A broken pencil who?
　　Ben: Never mind. It's pointless.
　　Skye: I don't think these jokes are helping your cause.
　　Ben: You love my jokes.
　　Skye: Meh.
　　Ben: Don't even try it. You used to tell me all the time how funny I was.
　　Skye: Was this in your dreams?
　　Ben: No. Yours. You talk in your sleep.
　　Skye: You're such a liar!
　　Ben: No way, Squeak. You're a fucking chatterbox.
　　Ben: We need to talk properly, Skye.
　　Skye: I'm not ready yet.
　　Ben: When?

Skye: Soon.

&a.

Thursday 10/19

Ben: Knock, knock.
    Skye: Who's there?
Ben: Aardvark.
    Skye: Aardvark who?
Ben: Aardvark a hundred miles for one of your smiles.
    Skye: *cough* lame *cough*
Ben: What's the longest word in the dictionary?
Skye: I don't know.
Ben: Smiles, because there is a mile between each S.
Ben: I miss seeing your smile.
Ben: Let's have dinner tomorrow night?
Skye: I need more time, Ben.
Ben: Squeak?
Skye: Yes?
Ben: I love you.

&a.

Monday 10/23

Ben: Knock, knock.
    Skye: Who's there?

Ben: Theodore.

Skye: Theodore who?

Ben: Theodore wasn't opened so I knocked.

Ben: I need the door to open, Squeak.

Ben: Or I can just kick the motherfucker down.

Skye: Lol.

Ben: I wish I was joking.

Skye: I'm getting there, Ben. Believe it or not, Cassidy is your biggest champion right now.

Ben: That's strange. The daily messages she's been sending me are all the varied and detailed ways she plans to remove my favorite body part.

Skye: And that's why I love her.

&

Friday 10/27

Ben: Knock, knock.

Skye: Who's there?

Ben: Cynthia.

Skye: Cynthia who?

Ben: Cynthia been away, I missed you.

Ben: I miss you.

Skye: I miss you too.

Ben: We need to talk, Squeak. We're not going to sort anything out by text.

Skye: I know.

Skye: Can you come around tomorrow at 7?

Ben: 7am? I'll be there.

Skye: Uh no, Mackinnon, 7pm.
Ben: You sure?
Skye: I'm sure.
Ben: Okay, I'll see you then.
Ben: Knock, knock.
Skye: Who's there?
Ben: Olive.
Skye: Olive who?
Ben: Olive you.
Skye: I love you too.

Looking at the clock as I dash madly around the apartment tidying it up, I see I have half an hour before Ben is due to arrive. The apartment doesn't actually need tidying, but I have so much nervous energy coursing through my body, I'm finding it impossible to sit still.

It's been three weeks since I last saw him, but he has been in contact daily, messaging me multiple times a day. Always starting with those ridiculous knock knock jokes. The ridiculous jokes that bring a smirk to my lips every time I think about them. I would never admit it to him, but I do love his humor, the way he doesn't take himself too seriously. So different to most men. So different to my father. Because he's not my father, he's a guy who loves me and who fucked up. A guy who has a past that scarred him, the same way my past bruised me. But he loves me, and he's sorry. I have complete confidence in that, and as soon as the realization hit me, I was almost desperate to see him. To touch him, reassure him. To love him.

The buzzer startles me out of my reverie. The clock tells me that Ben is early, and I don't think I have ever been so grateful for his impatience. Buzzing him in, I move to the door and wait for his knock, practically vibrating with anticipation.

It feels like an eternity has passed with no sign of his arrival, and in a moment of frustration I wrench the door open, coming face to face with Ben, his arm raised, and I have to duck down to miss the knock that almost lands on my forehead.

"Shit, Skye, sorry. Are you okay?" he asks, leaning forward. Grabbing hold of me, his eyes map my face, ensuring he didn't make contact, while a laugh escapes me. Of all the ways I imagined this going, that was definitely not one of them.

"I'm fine," I answer and as his eyes finally land on mine. I feel the last shred of indecision take flight. This man is it for me.

Throwing myself at him, Ben is caught off guard, but he still manages to catch me. And there's not a doubt in my mind that he will always be the one to catch me.

I reach for him mindlessly, my hands needing to touch him, for his solid strength to anchor me. Our mouths clash as Ben drags my body against his, moving me forward so he can enter. I hear the door slam, but my eyes remain closed as I enjoy every sensation that his touch inspires in me.

Turning us around, Ben slams me into the door, his

body completely flush with mine, as though he can't possibly get close enough. Breaking the kiss, he pulls back slightly, and I can sense his apprehension.

"Are we going to be okay, Squeak?"

I take his face in my hands as I consider how to answer. "We are going to be a perfect chaotic mess of imperfection," I reply, and remembering Wyatt's words to me all those months ago, I continue, "we're going to let the happiness bring us to our knees."

Ben places a soft kiss on my mouth, licking along my bottom lip before biting down gently.

"I do like you on your knees," he rasps out with a wicked glint in his eye.

"You're such a pervert!" I laugh out, before he shuts me up with a kiss that is all tongue and teeth, licking and biting.

Grabbing my ass, he lifts me with ease, squeezing my cheeks with no regard for gentleness, and I love it. His rough touch causes my pussy to clench, and I grind myself against him in an attempt to get the friction my clit so fiercely needs. With a low chuckle that sends a shiver through me, Ben asks, "You want my cock, baby?"

"Fuck yes," I answer, with not a hint of hesitation.

"Ah, see now, what are we going to do about that filthy mouth, Squeak? You might need to be punished." His lips find my neck, chasing a harsh bite, with a tender kiss.

"Promises, promises," I sigh.

Suddenly and without warning, I am hoisted over Ben's shoulder into a fireman's hold, and the sound of his large hand cracking across my rounded ass echoes throughout the room.

"Don't say I didn't warn you, Squeak," he says as he strides briskly across the apartment, heading straight for my bedroom, where he spends the next few hours fucking me, and loving me in equal measures.

I lie in bed the following morning watching the sunrise through the sheer curtains, completely overwhelmed with my happiness. The road we took to get to this moment was rocky, and there were moments I definitely feared we wouldn't make it. But lying here with the steady drum of Ben's heartbeat playing under my ear, and his hard, sinewy chest beneath my fingertips I am sure that every bump, every stumble, every faltered step was worth it. Would continue to be worth it.

Turning my head, I place a kiss on Ben's shoulder, careful not to wake him; and as I close my eyes to chase the slumber that has eluded me, I send out a silent prayer of thanks to whatever entity exists out there, for bringing me exactly what I didn't realize I needed. I guess the dick-pic gods had my back after all.

BEN

Five years later

There are people everywhere I turn, and I am seriously going to lose my shit if this party doesn't get started soon. The sooner it starts, the sooner it ends, and the sooner I can lay my girl out beneath me and watch her face as she comes apart under my fingers. My mouth. My cock. I feel my dick start to thicken at the memory of her ass bent over the sofa last night. Her back arched as I fisted a handful of hair, that juicy ass marked pink by the crack of my hand, and her eyes glazed with lust as she held my gaze over her shoulder. Fuck, I need to put this shit on lockdown unless I want to be sporting a giant hard-on at truly the most inappropriate moment.

Mason steps forward from his spot next to me with a ridiculous smirk on his face, and my impending boner deflates immediately.

"You alright there, man? You look like you're about to bust out of your skin."

"Yeah, I'm good. I just need this fucking party to start already. Five years is a long time to wait."

Five years. I shake my head in disbelief. It was never supposed to take this long. But life, man. It has a way of giving you exactly what you need, before you realize you need it.

"I wouldn't let Skye hear you refer to this as a 'party', she'll kick your ass." Mason laughs but I shrug it off. I love Squeak's feistiness as much as I love her sweetness, and any ass kicking she wants to give is just fine with me. God knows I take plenty of liberties with her ass.

My attention is drawn to the crowd up ahead as some sort of commotion appears to be happening. Suddenly a flash of pink bolts through the legs of the upstanding adults, and I spot the curly-haired demon that is my daughter running up the path, headed straight toward me. However, she pulls up comedically short when she spots Sebastian, her best friend, standing beside his Grandmother, and the three-year-olds throw themselves into each other's arms, as if they haven't seen each other in months. I roll my eyes. I'm pretty sure it's been about forty-five minutes.

Turning to Mason, I bite out, "We're in trouble with those two, aren't we?" But his answering chuckle does little to calm my worries.

"Summer!" I holler across the crowd, and her bright green eyes, so much like her mother's, meet mine.

"What, Daddy?!" Summer hollers right back.

Holding back a smile, I consider, not for the first time, how much of her mother's sassiness she has also inherited.

"Come here, Sass!" As her little legs propel her forward, I notice my father and Fiona following her down the path, but before I can greet them, Summer throws herself at me, wrapping her arms around my neck, and leaning in to whisper something in my ear.

"Daddy, guess what?"

"What?" I reply conspiratorially.

"Seb said he's gonna marry me one day!" Her excited whisper carries, and I hear Mason snort out a laugh beside me, while I try to muffle my groan.

"Here you go, Ben." My father arrives next to us, my youngest daughter wriggling in his arms, reaching out for me. Shifting Summer to my other side, I extend my left arm and take hold of Poppy, who immediately lies her head on my shoulder and lets her eyes flutter shut.

Looking at my girls in my arms, I marvel at their differences. Poppy is the calm in the storm, while Summer is usually the storm. And I wouldn't change either of them for anything.

My phone vibrates in my back pocket, so I place Summer on the ground, and reach around to pull it out. Seeing Cassidy's name light up the screen, I put the phone to my ear and answer with a short, "Yeah?"

"We're here, fady, send the monkeys up to the entrance," she demands.

"Oka– wait, what the fuck is a fady, Alexander?"

"Well, let's just say, I finally got Skyballs to admit

something last night." She sniggers like a schoolgirl, much to my chagrin.

"I probably don't want to know, right?"

"Ugh, dude, look it up on urban dictionary, 'kay? We don't have time for this shit right now! Send the rugrats up to us, so we can get this party started."

I hear some rustling in the background, followed by the unmistakable voice of Squeak. "Jesus, can you please not refer to my wedding as a party, Cass?"

I laugh, and for the first time since she kicked me out of her hotel room last night, the tension leaves my shoulders.

"Dad and Fiona will be there in a minute with all of them. Put her on the phone, will you?"

"No, I will not put her on the phone, Captain America! Christ, you can wait five minu—"

"Ben?" Skye's voice fills my ear as Mason takes Poppy from me, and I see him help Dad round up the kids.

"Hey, Squeak, you ready to do this, baby?"

"Yes," she says with a sigh. "I've been ready to do this for five years, baby cakes. It's time to finally make an honest woman out of me."

"As long as I can still make a slutty woman out of you tonight."

Her giggle echoes through the phone line and I grin at the sound, already planning all the filthy things I'm going to do to her tonight.

"Still such a pervert after all these years! Okay, Mackinnon, I've gotta go, I'm getting married in five minutes."

"You are? Well damn, he's a lucky guy, Squeak," I retort softly.

"I'll see you in a minute, okay? Our babies are here." Before I can reply, Skye's voice is replaced by Cassidy's.

"Okay, see you soon, stud muffin. Kiss, kiss." She hangs up on me.

Shaking my head at her audaciousness, I watch as the celebrant begins to organize the congregated group in preparation for Squeak's entrance.

Once everyone is seated, I hear the acoustic guitar start, and the first strains of Songbird begin. Turning my attention to the path leading up Cherry Esplanade, I watch in silence as first Layla, then Wyatt and Cassidy follow the path until they're standing alongside us.

Then my girls are there, making their way to me. I don't see the dress, or the makeup. I just see her, and for the millionth time I realize what a lucky son of a bitch I am, that this woman is mine.

Mine to love. Mine to adore. Mine to fuck.

After what seems like an e-fucking-ternity, she is standing in front of me, and I can't stop myself from moving toward her, closing the gap between us. I never could stand not to be touching her. Leaning over, I pick up Summer and move my body flush against Skye's, placing my hand over hers on Poppy's back and leaning my forehead against hers.

I'm oblivious to the people around us. To the celebrant waiting to begin our ceremony. To everything and everyone.

"Hey, Squeak."

"Hey, you," she whispers.

Closing my eyes, I inhale this memory, determined to remember every moment of it.

"Knock, knock."

"Who's there?"

"Juno."

"Juno who?"

"Juno I love you, right?"

And as she huffs out a soft laugh, I take her mouth in a kiss that is as all-consuming as she is.

I hope you enjoyed *Under the Cherry Blossoms*! Keep reading for a sneak peek at book 2 in the Finding Forever series, *Dandelion Dreams* (Cassidy's story!), and please consider leaving a review.

***

If you would like to read more from Ben & Skye, you can grab their bonus short story The Pick-Up Artist (previously published in the Take Me To Bed Anthology) HERE!

***

Would you like a FREE book?
Get your copy of Rule Breaker, a steamy student/teacher rom com, HERE!

Nine Years Ago

My phone buzzes in my hand and I roll my eyes, laughing when I see Aidan's name on the screen. I knew he wouldn't make it through the night without calling me. Such a loser.

My loser, though.

Answering the phone with my patented Aidan greeting, "Whaddup, Boner." I hear Aidan Bonefield sigh in exasperation.

"Christ, CJ, I have to deal with that shit all the time, shouldn't my girlfriend cut me some slack?"

"Are you fucking kidding me, Boner? It's my obligation as your girlfriend to torment you with this as much as possible! Now what do you want? My girls and I are about to go get our slut on. Skye's giving me the stink eye as we speak."

I cover the receiver and glare right back at my best friend, Skye.

"Calm your juicy tits, Skyeballs, give me five minutes to deal with my Boner!" I return to my conversation with Aidan.

"CJ, what the hell do you mean 'get your slut on'?" Aidan bites out.

"Jesus, Boner, relax, it's just an expression. What do you want anyway? You're supposed to be off getting alcohol poisoning with your idiot friends."

I hear him laugh, and I swear if I had a heart, it would skip a beat. That velvety chuckle is my undoing and has me dropping my panties more often than is probably appropriate.

"Have you been up to your room since I left?"

"Nope, I got dressed in Devon's room so I could steal her clothes. Why?"

"I left something for you."

I can practically feel my eyes light up. There's nothing I like better than a surprise. Well, I mean, except orgasms, but then who doesn't love a good orgasm?

Making my way up the stairs to my room on the second floor of the dorm, I hear the muffled sounds of Aidan's loser friends in the background, and try to control my irritation. How he puts up with them I have no clue.

"Where are you guys?"

"In the car, heading to Smiley's. Jackson's our DD tonight and the asswipe won't stop bitching about it."

I snort out a laugh as I reach my door. Jackson is the

biggest douchedick around, so I find his misery highly enjoyable. Opening the door to my room I make my way inside when I hear a loud screech followed by a variety of expletives.

"Aidan? Aidan, what happened? Are you there?" I bark out the words and the anxiety in my voice is clear.

"You dickwad! Be fucking careful, asshole. Fuck! You know the roads are icy, you prick."

My heart rate returns to normal as I hear Aidan's strong voice cursing out someone, presumably Jackson.

"You okay there, Boner?"

"Yeah, we're good."

"Okay, well, tell Jackson the jackass I'm going to kick his ass next time I see him, for scaring me like that."

Huffing out a laugh he replies, "Yeah, I'm sure he'll be terrified, Blondie." He pauses for effect before continuing, "are you in your room yet?"

"Yep." I glance around, looking for my surprise, but seeing nothing. I'm unable to hide the disappointment in my voice. "There's nothing here! Are you screwing with me, Boner? You do remember who grants you access to the pussy parade, don't you?"

"The bed, CJ, check the bed." I can practically feel the exasperation vibrating in his voice.

Moving forward, I spot the treasure lying on my pillow.

"Aidan." My voice is barely a whisper, missing its usual bravado.

"You like it?"

I bend over and pick up the small bouquet of

dandelions he left for me. Bringing the delicate flowers to my nose, I inhale deeply, and I'm immediately over-whelmed with memories from my childhood. These flowers—my favorites—are so meaningful to me. I love that Aidan understands that this little bouquet is going to endear him to me, so much more than any big money item.

"They're beautiful, Aidan, I love…."

"FUCK!" A strangled cry from Aidan cuts me off, and my stomach plummets. The blatant terror in his voice reaches through the phone line and wraps an icy cold grip around my heart. "Aidan!" I scream as my ears are assaulted with the sound of screeching tires and splintering glass. The usual arrogant tones of boys who are still growing into men, are replaced with shrill cries of fear and panic, before an eerie silence descends, broken only by the occasional creak of mutilated metal. The dandelions drop to the floor, petals scattering.

"AIDAN!"

CASSIDY

*F*ucking, fuckity, fuckbomb.

My hand flies up to tuck a strand of blonde hair behind my ear, but instead it begins to unconsciously twirl the silky tendril around my finger.

Breathe in. One. Two. Three. Breathe out. One. Two. Three.

"Miss. Jensen, are you listening to me?" Glancing up, I meet the watery, blue eyes of the Human Resources Manager and attempt to control the expletives that are sitting on the tip of my tongue, just waiting to burst forth.

"Yes, I am, sir." I endeavor to sound as meek as possible. No matter how much it pains me, I need to recover this situation and turn it around. I refuse to believe this cannot be fixed. "Mr. Connors, let me assure you that I could not be more sorry for my behavior, and I guarantee that it will never happen again." Mustering all the fake sincerity I have in me, I look across the desk and bestow a blindingly bright smile on him. Taking in the weathered, lined face of the man sitting across from me, I can't help but notice how his weary appearance is in stark contrast to the vibrancy with which I try to live my life. I do my best not to cringe as I can almost feel his apathy rub off on me.

"Miss. Jensen, you fell asleep in a meeting. A meeting where you were a representative of this firm, and in turn, presented us in a highly unprofessional manner." Sighing loudly, he rubs his eyes roughly. "Quite frankly, the crass and uncouth behavior you have demonstrated since your employment, has been appalling. You have already received three written warnings, and I'm afraid I have no choice but to let you go."

My mouth drops open in surprise. Suddenly time slows down, and my senses are heightened. I hear the ticking of Connors' wall clock, the rasp of his breath as he awaits my response. I feel the sweat break out across my brow and my heart jumps to my throat. This can't be happening, plays on a loop in my head. As awful as this job is, I need it.

"Conn- uh, I... Mr. Connors, look, I'm sure we can work something out. I agree totally that my behavior was unacceptable, and I can fully accept the need for disciplinary action, but surely dismissal is unnecessary. I mean, if I hadn't had that dream and gotten a little...um, noisy, no one would have even noticed my little nap!"

The derisive noise that escapes him, tells me that

Connors isn't buying what I'm selling. Not a problem, I just need to lay it on a little thicker.

"Mr. Connors, sir, what if I agree to unpaid overtime for a month? Or, or a week of unpaid leave where I think about my behavior and—"

"This is not a negotiation, I'm sorry." Walking around his desk, he takes a seat, steepling his fingers in front of him, and meeting my eye. "Please gather your personal items from your desk, and leave the premises, Miss. Jensen. You can collect your reference letter at the front desk on your way out." Leaning back in his chair, Connors sizes me up, and for the first time since I entered his office, I sense a tiny bit of empathy. "Your administrative work here was adequate, Cassidy, and while your attitude isn't a fit for Patterson & Partners, I'm sure you will be an asset somewhere else. Perhaps in a less rigid environment. All of which has been reflected in your reference letter."

I'm still staring at him, slack jawed, as I try to make sense of what is happening. I hate this job. I've hated every office job I've ever had. But I have never once been fired from a job. People love me! I'm a fucking delight.

"That will be all, Miss. Jensen."

I realize that I am, once again, being dismissed, so I gather myself as best as I can, and begin to make my exit.

Stopping in the doorway, I slowly turn, formulating my words and deciding what I want his last impression of me to be. Classy, I decide. Classy is the smart option.

Nah, fuck that.

"Connors, dude, everyone knows that's a fucking rug on your head. And it's not even a good one. It's like an animal crawled up there, got cozy, and decided it was a good place to die. You really should do something about that, if you want people to take you seriously. Toodles!" Turning on my heel, I sashay out of the office, smirking at the sounds of indignation that follow me.

Sitting on a stool, I lean back, placing my elbows on the counter behind me, and survey my surroundings. Crossing my legs, I let my heel slip and dangle from my right foot, bouncing it carelessly. Monroe's is bustling with the dinner-time rush, and while I normally enjoy people-watching, tonight the raised voices and almost frenzied atmosphere is straining my nerves.

Glancing down at my watch I see that Wyatt will be finishing up her shift in a few minutes, and Skye should be arriving any time now. My eyes scan the diner again, falling on a booth containing three teenage boys. They've been sucking down water for the past twenty minutes, and I'm ready to pounce as soon as they vacate their prime spot. The lanky, spotted one wearing a backwards baseball cap looks up and catches my eye. Leveling him with my best scowl, I throw him daggers that would put Regina George to shame. He cowers for a moment, before hastily grabbing up his things and urging his friends to do the same. In the blink of an eye, they're scam-

Connors isn't buying what I'm selling. Not a problem, I just need to lay it on a little thicker.

"Mr. Connors, sir, what if I agree to unpaid overtime for a month? Or, or a week of unpaid leave where I think about my behavior and—"

"This is not a negotiation, I'm sorry." Walking around his desk, he takes a seat, steepling his fingers in front of him, and meeting my eye. "Please gather your personal items from your desk, and leave the premises, Miss. Jensen. You can collect your reference letter at the front desk on your way out." Leaning back in his chair, Connors sizes me up, and for the first time since I entered his office, I sense a tiny bit of empathy. "Your administrative work here was adequate, Cassidy, and while your attitude isn't a fit for Patterson & Partners, I'm sure you will be an asset somewhere else. Perhaps in a less rigid environment. All of which has been reflected in your reference letter."

I'm still staring at him, slack jawed, as I try to make sense of what is happening. I hate this job. I've hated every office job I've ever had. But I have never once been fired from a job. People love me! I'm a fucking delight.

"That will be all, Miss. Jensen."

I realize that I am, once again, being dismissed, so I gather myself as best as I can, and begin to make my exit.

Stopping in the doorway, I slowly turn, formulating my words and deciding what I want his last impression of me to be. Classy, I decide. Classy is the smart option.

Nah, fuck that.

"Connors, dude, everyone knows that's a fucking rug on your head. And it's not even a good one. It's like an animal crawled up there, got cozy, and decided it was a good place to die. You really should do something about that, if you want people to take you seriously. Toodles!" Turning on my heel, I sashay out of the office, smirking at the sounds of indignation that follow me.

Sitting on a stool, I lean back, placing my elbows on the counter behind me, and survey my surroundings. Crossing my legs, I let my heel slip and dangle from my right foot, bouncing it carelessly. Monroe's is bustling with the dinner-time rush, and while I normally enjoy people-watching, tonight the raised voices and almost frenzied atmosphere is straining my nerves.

Glancing down at my watch I see that Wyatt will be finishing up her shift in a few minutes, and Skye should be arriving any time now. My eyes scan the diner again, falling on a booth containing three teenage boys. They've been sucking down water for the past twenty minutes, and I'm ready to pounce as soon as they vacate their prime spot. The lanky, spotted one wearing a backwards baseball cap looks up and catches my eye. Leveling him with my best scowl, I throw him daggers that would put Regina George to shame. He cowers for a moment, before hastily grabbing up his things and urging his friends to do the same. In the blink of an eye, they're scampering out the door, and I throw myself into the booth.

Grabbing the menu, my eyes slide over the options without really taking anything in. My mind is still in turmoil, trying to assess the damage from today. One thing is blindingly obvious though; I need to find a new job as soon as possible. If my dream is to ever get off the ground, I need to have an income to help finance it. And for all the boring shit too, I guess. A gal really does need food in her belly, and a roof over her head.

My mind starts to mentally scan through my professional contacts, trying to remember if I'd heard of any jobs going recently. Working in an office is as boring as fuck, so I try to keep things interesting by changing jobs often. This means I've managed to gain some inside sources over the years. However, this is the first time I have ever needed a new job, rather than just looking for a way to alleviate my boredom.

"Hey, Sweetie."

I startle comedically as Wyatt slides into the booth opposite me.

"Jesus fucking Christ, Red! Are you trying to kill me?"

Snickering, she rolls her eyes in response to my dramatic statement, but fuck. She just took years off my life!

"How long until Skye gets here? I'm starving."

"She shouldn't be very long. We both know what she'll get though, so we may as well put the order in." I let my eyes scan the menu one last time. Still nothing seems appetizing, so I settle on a tuna melt.

"Okay, I'll run up and give our orders to Dylan."

I watch Wyatt as she makes her way to the kitchen, all long limbs, swaying ass and graceful strides. She maneuvers through the crowd with ease, and I envy how content she seems here. Sometimes it feels like I'll never find my place in this world. Damned if I don't keep trying though.

"Ugh." Skye appears as if from nowhere and takes up a seat alongside me.

"What the fuck is up with you two scaring the shit out of me?!"

Skye fumbles with her purse, pushing me further along and getting herself situated before looking at me incredulously. "Are you serious right now? I said your name about a thousand times before I sat down, asking you to move!"

"A thousand?" I let the word fall from my mouth disbelievingly. "Well, you know, Balls, I'm glad to see you're not prone to exaggeration. I'd hate to think that Spanky wasn't really sporting an eight-inch cock."

"Cassidy! Oh my god, I have never once told you how big Ben's mmm-hmm is!"

My eyes practically pop out of my head and, as hard as I try, I can't stop the loud snort of laughter that escapes me.

Wyatt chooses this moment to return to the booth and looks between the two of us quizzically, one eyebrow raised. "Do I even want to know?"

"No." Skye's voice is firm and brokers no argument, so I roll my eyes and mouth "later" to Wyatt, which causes her to giggle. Yeah, Wyatt's a giggler. Nobody's perfect, I guess.

"Okay, why are we here, Cass?" Skye turns her attention to me, and in a very uncommon reaction, I feel my cheeks start to pink.

"I got fired today." My words are uttered with far more confidence than I'm actually feeling, and I'm pretty damn proud that I got it out without a single waver.

Looking up, I am met with two shocked expressions, their eyes almost as wide as their mouths.

"Well, say something! Isn't this where you're supposed to offer me encouragement and tell me how everything is going to be all right?" I swing my head between my two best friends. "I've gotta say, I'm pretty disappointed in you both right now."

Skye is the first to regain control of her verbal capabilities, spewing out a bunch of platitudes while grabbing my hand in both of hers and squeezing tight. Which I'm sure is supposed to be comforting, but the reality is more excruciating than anything else.

"Cassidy, what happened?" Wyatt's voice is quietly curious, but manages to avoid any sense of attack. I think we all know that my work ethic can sometimes leave a lot to be desired, so I appreciate the restraint she's showing.

"I might have fallen asleep in a meeting." The grip on my hand loosens, and I can sense that I'm losing my audience, so I rush on. "But in my defence, I had been up the entire night before, getting an order finished. And nobody would have even realized I was asleep, but

I started having that recurring Chris Pratt dream. You know the one where he's licking my—" Noticing the raised eyebrows and unimpressed looks I am receiving from my "friends" I decide it's best to cut that thought short. "Anyway, all I'm saying is I made a few little moans, and suddenly I'm unemployable? How is that fair?"

Skye and Wyatt look at each other across the table, and I try to gauge their reactions. I'm aware that napping during an important meeting is probably not the most professional thing I've ever done. But, Christ, being an administrative assistant, for a taxation lawyer no less, is boring as all fuck. Surely concessions need to be made to accommodate the boredom factor?

"You fell asleep during a meeting?" Skye's voice is brimming with barely concealed mirth. I nod my head solemnly. "So, to clarify, you fell asleep during a meeting, and then while you were asleep, you had a dirty dream about Chris Pratt—during which time, you made sex noises. And let's be clear, I was your roommate for four years, I know that your sex noises are loud and proud. That would have been quite... the aural delight for a bunch of middle-aged tax accountants, Cass." Wyatt slaps a hand over her mouth in what I assume is an attempt to hide the unattractive snort laugh that follows Skye's statement.

"Okay, it wasn't my finest moment, I am fully prepared to admit that. But I really think that thundercunt, Connors, overreacted. I mean if anything, a woman of my stature giving the old hornballs a show like that, would have helped them get that account."

"A woman of your stature?" Wyatt enquires.

"Yes, Red," I answer, trying to keep the exasperation from my voice. "I am young and hot, therefore of a high stature." I turn to Skye. "That works, yeah?" Her only response is a sigh.

"What are you going to do, Cass? Do you have any savings? You can always come and stay with Ben and I." I cringe at the thought. As much as I love my best friend, and as much as I love tormenting her boyfriend, staying with the recently reconciled couple is not in my plans.

"Thanks for the offer, Skyeballs, and as much as I would love to stay with the bonk buddies, if I was going to crash with anyone, it would be Red over here," I respond, pointing my finger at Wyatt.

Her eyes widen in surprise, with just a tiny hint of horror. To be honest, I'm slightly offended.

"Oh, yeah, of course, Sweetie. You can stay with me as long as you like."

"Relax, Wyatt." I let her off the hook. "I have the money that I was saving for a new oven. I'm good for a couple of months at least." Sighing, I finally allow the strain of today to wash over me, and my shoulders slump.

"Maybe you should take this as a sign, Cassidy." I glance up at Wyatt, as Skye sucks in a breath and starts bouncing in her seat.

"Yesssss, Cass! This is it! It's time for you to start focusing on your business! With no day job distracting you, you can start taking on more baking jobs. You've been wanting to do this for years, killing yourself to get orders done around work hours. This is perfect!" She claps her hands, practically giddy.

"Slow your roll there, Balls. That "distraction" pays the bills, you know." My brain is scrambling, trying to come up with a valid reason why I couldn't try to kick-start my business. You know, other than because I'm scared shitless of failing. Because scared is the one thing I will never admit to being.

"It's not that easy, my schnookums. Every chick and her cute little fluffy dog has a cupcake business these days. It would take months, fuck maybe even years, to get something off the ground, let alone something successful enough that I could quit working." I lean back in the booth and take in my girls' eager faces.

"Goddammit, if I have to be the voice of reason here, we're in a fuckload of trouble, you realize that, right?"

Skye tilts her head to the side, a cute little mannerism she has when she's thinking, and carefully considers everything I have said.

"What if you could find some part-time office work, you know, a few days a week, and then you could bake the rest of the week?"

I consider this seriously. It would be great to have more time to take on extra orders. I have a small group of loyal customers who are constantly referring people to me, I just haven't had the time to say yes to them. And I would still have the safety net of a secure, paying job (as long as I could manage to stay awake from now on, that is).

"That might work," I say slowly. "It actually might

be perfect." The tension starts to evaporate as I feel myself settling into this idea, and my stomach comes alive, rumbling loudly.

"Ugh, where's our food, Red? I'm starving!" My eyes scan the diner, and I release a little shriek when I see Brenda, who is working the dinner shift, headed our way with a tray full of food.

"Just a heads up, you biatches are buying me dinner tonight; we're celebrating." Holding up my water glass, I raise it high. "Cheers to Mr. Pratt and his talented dream tongue. Without whom, this opportunity never would have been thrust upon me. Much like his tongue thrust—"

"Lalalalalala." Wyatt covers her ears.

"We get the idea!" Skye shrieks.

"Jesus, when did you girls get so prudish? Fine," I raise my glass once again, "here's to part-time work. May it be easy to find, and even easier to stay awake through."

Dandelion Dreams is **AVAILABLE NOW!**

Stay Connected

Private Facebook Group: https://www.facebook.com/groups/amalisrisqueromantics
BookBub: https://www.bookbub.com/authors/amali-rose
Facebook: https://www.facebook.com/authoramalirose
Goodreads: https://www.goodreads.com/author/show/17064277.Amali_Rose
Instagram: https://www.instagram.com/authoramalirose
TikTok: https://vm.tiktok.com/ZS3KAon3/

My newsletter is the best way to stay in contact with me! You'll get first look at titles, covers and release dates, plus exclusive sneak peeks!
Sign up here: https://tinyurl.com/y6h3hw9s

More by Amali Rose

Finding Forever Series
(Standalone series)

Under the Cherry Blossoms >> Fling to Forever
Romance
Dandelion Dreams >> Enemies to Lovers/Office
Romance
Amongst the Wildflowers >> Friends to Lovers
Romance
Breathing Wisteria >> Second Chance Romance
<u>Finding Forever</u> >> The Complete Series

Greetings From Avondale Series
(Standalone Series)

Mistletoe Mistake >> Brother's Best Friend/Holiday
Romance
Miss Independent >> Billionaire Romance

Standalones:

Dating the DILF >> Single Dad Romantic Comedy

ACKNOWLEDGMENTS

Firstly, to every single person who took a chance on a new author and read this book, you have my eternal gratitude. I wish I could give every one of you a giant bear hug! Publishing this book terrified me, but the support I have received has been overwhelming and humbling. Thank you all so much.

To my alpha & beta readers: Joz, Kimberly, Harper, Tanya, Stacey, Rachel, Tamara, Tre, Laura, Lauren, Devon, Ashley, Cheril, Kim & Brenda. Your feedback, opinions and support all helped to make this book what it is. I valued every word, every message and every bit of kindness. I hope I made you a little bit proud.

Special shout out to Tre for her New York knowledge!

Joz, there are no words. I will be forever grateful that I found you. Thank you for your endless patience with my questions and your unwavering belief that I could do this. I can honestly say this book wouldn't have been written if it hadn't been for your support, encouragement & kindness. I love you hard!

Rachel, you have been my biggest cheerleader from the very start, and I can't thank you enough. The belief you have shown in me and the enthusiasm with which you have supported me, has meant everything, and I'm so lucky to call you my friend.

Tanya, you were the first person I confided this dream in, the first person to tell me I could do it. You encouraged me when I wanted to give up and you believed in me when when I didn't believe in myself. I love your guts!

The Sassy ladies! Joz, Kim, Stacey, Harper, Sienna & Laura. You guys took me under your wing and are the epitome of what the indie community is about. Thank you all for the encouragement and support you have given me, I'm so incredibly grateful to you all.

Ben Ellis, working with you is a delight! Thank you for creating such a gorgeous cover for me!

Stacey & Petrina at Spell Bound, thank you for all your hard work editing this book for me. You were an absolute pleasure to work with and you truly made my story better.

To my street team, Amali's Sinful Sweethearts:
Antonette, Cassy, Devon, Heather, Katrina, Kristi,
Lauren, Rachel, Tamara & Tre. The support you guys
show me, and the time you spend sharing my work
humbles me. I am unbelievably grateful that I have you
incredible women in my corner. Thank you for
everything!

To my amazing friends Kerry & Karen.
*"There is nothing I would not do for those who are really my
friends. I have no notion of loving people by halves, it is not
in my nature"* ~ Jane Austen.

All the wonderful people in my reader's group, Amali's
Risque Romantics. You all took a chance on a new
author and I love you for that. I have so enjoyed getting
to know you all and I look forward to more smutty
goodness in the future!

Finally, to all the incredible bloggers who read,
reviewed and shared Under The Cherry Blossoms. I
understand how important the job you do is, and I
cannot thank you enough for all of your hard work,
and the love you have shown my story. From the
bottom of my heart, thank you!

Huge love and hugs!
Amali xox

ABOUT THE AUTHOR

USA Today Bestselling author Amali Rose is a former blogger from Australia, who released her debut novella in 2017.

A self confessed bookworm, her love affair with the written word began as a child, with *The Magic Faraway Tree*. Her tastes have grown and evolved over the years and, after stumbling into the indie community a few years ago, she discovered her passion for romance with a side of smut.

When not reading or writing, Amali enjoys cheesy pop music, netflix marathons, and she believes strongly that pink, puppies and chocolate make the world a better place!